AMBER DUST

Jil Plummer

Andrew Benzie Books
Orinda, California

Published by Andrew Benzie Books
www.andrewbenziebooks.com

Printed in the United States of America

First Edition: Ferbuary 2014

10 9 8 7 6 5 4 3 2 1

ISBN 978-0-9897584-2-0

www.jilplummer.com

Cover and book design by Andrew Benzie

Cover Image by Robert Plummer
www.bobbertwp.blogspot.com

For Seamus and Cappuccino
my furry, patient companions

PROLOGUE

Memory freezes the dead in immortal perfection while the living remain to be faulted.

Andrea learned this fact later, but from the very first she understood that Robert James was only interested in her because she listened so raptly to reminiscences of his beloved fiancée, the wild and beautiful Lesley Clayton. This magical creature had died tragically the day before their wedding and the story, set in the distant Yorkshire Dales, seemed so wonderfully romantic to the adoring twenty-year-old Californian that being Robert's second choice became a privilege. With all her heart Andrea promised God, and herself, that she would endure anything if only she could have Robert for her husband.

Her wish came true but, after their marriage, Andrea's feelings toward Lesley began to change. The effort of keeping her contract grew into an obsession that transformed her from sensitive dreamer to hard-driving perfectionist. In time she had no feelings at all.

Now, twenty years later, Robert was dead.

CHAPTER ONE

The organ boomed, moaned, sobbed and sighed.

St. Stephen's nave resembled the belly of a great whale, showing ribs of bare wood and allowing flashes of daylight only when doors opened to let mourners in like schools of minnow, to slip about until they found somewhere to settle. Rustles, coughs and whispers caused wavelets of movement, and flowers massed around the large casket gave off a scent close to decay.

Each person, immediately after being seated, searched for "the family" in the front pew.

"Look, there's his wife! Doesn't look particularly upset, does she?"

"Wouldn't want to spoil her makeup."

"Don't have to be catty. Isn't that their son beside her? 'Bout seventeen, isn't he? Don't see him much, always off at that boarding school."

"Too bad; the girls'd love to meet him. Good looking kid."

"Like his dad."

"Lucky if he's half as successful."

A church full of critics approved as the boy shifted position and bowed his head, but most condemned his mother for being so controlled, shoulders square, evincing no hint of grief; living up to the nickname of Her Ladyship. She had been dubbed long ago by one of the many who had been affronted by her coldness.

Whispering continued like whistles and gurgles of digestion.

"Better if she'd stayed home with Robert a bit. Can't remember when I've seen them together."

"Never heard him complain. Never looked at another woman either, so far as anyone knows."

"Worked himself to an early grave."

"Left her rich."

Attention peaked as a choked sob arose but the movement of a white handkerchief proved it to be one of the two older women who sat on the other side of the boy. An odd pair. Small, wiry and, as always, dressed in shapeless muddy brown garments, they were known to neighborhood children as the "witches." They had appeared at the James house annually since anyone could remember so were believed to be some kind of relative. No one had ever felt it acceptable to ask, although they couldn't have said why.

"They got here from England quickly enough."

"Bad pennies. Never did like 'em. Shh, It's starting."

The minister began with a short prayer and during the Amen when he glanced down at the widow's face he was surprised to see complete calm, even disinterest. This would never do. He gathered himself for a greater effort. It would take work to stir this one. He measured the success of his eulogies by tears tapped from the most unemotional of his congregation, and so far he had never failed. All for their own good, of course.

He took a deep breath, doubled his chin for his most resonant tones, and launched into his best effort at cloaking Robert in all the virtues the dead so often and so easily accrue.

"Friends. We are here to mourn the passing of a fine and generous man, Robert James. A man of humor and kindness, a man who helped all he came in contact with and, above all, a man who loved his family…"

Love. Love. Fool's talk, thought Andrea feeling slightly nauseated as the minister's voice rose and fell, resounding from the timbers then purring among the shadows, lurking to pounce again on sensibilities that longed only for peace.

She would not listen. She turned her gaze to where her husband's nose protruded like a grotesque stamen from behind the petals of a purple tulip. She had said goodbye to him that morning at the mortuary, in a small room like a Motel Six. It had been so long since they had spoken, other than the necessities of everyday living and short discussions while reading the daily paper with its impending wars and present disasters, that now there was nothing to say to him dead. She had not even allowed herself to think as she looked at his expressionless face. Once or twice when sentimental thoughts threatened to break through, the protection she had forged through so many years had not let her down. He could have been a stranger. Robert was a stranger.

A terrible ache gripped Andrea's throat and she forced her attention to a rough patch on the strap of her handbag, the hairs that bristled from the minister's ears, and finally she immersed herself in plans for the Cancer Society's fund raising dinner.

The service ended about the time she'd decided how to handle the publicity, and then she was allowed to walk toward the side door away from the minister's disappointment, the flowers, the coffin, and whoever it was who lay in it.

"And did those feet in ancient times walk upon England's mountains green…" Her husband's favorite hymn, which she vaguely remembered requesting, boomed out triumphantly, almost derisively, chasing her as she gasped in the fresh air and rushed her surprised son to their car. "Let's get home," she said. "I'll drive."

Critical faces watched Robert's silver BMW accelerate down the road and make a right without even hesitating at the stop sign.

"She didn't visit the casket at all. How odd."

"Disgusting if you ask me."

"Not a flicker of grief. Heartless. Well, I always did think her a cold fish."

"And he doted on her so."

With satisfaction in their hearts, those who were considered friends of the family prepared to leave for the James' house and refreshments.

CHAPTER TWO

Andrea looked around the crowded room and saw that everyone had a drink and most were munching happily from the plates of dainty catered sandwiches, sliced meats, cheeses, cookies and cakes.

"You forgot us."

Her nose pinching at the smell of mothballs, Andrea looked down into Effie's accusing, beady eyes.

"And the chauffeur. You're not supposed to drive yourself at funerals." Agnes peered up from beside her sister, veined cheeks even ruddier than usual.

"Aye, we had to take a lift with yon Merrimans. Felt right daft."

Andrea felt the old revulsion for these two crones who had hovered like vultures over her marriage but, as was her habit, she swallowed words like bile and produced as near to politeness as she could, "I'm very sorry. I suppose I forgot. I had to get home to prepare…"

They stood there, staring.

Suddenly a wonderful thought came to Andrea. Soon she'd be free of them forever. With Robert gone they'd have no reason to ever speak to her again!

She swept a glass of champagne from a passing tray and took a sip, then paused. Did they usually serve champagne at funerals? Odd. The bubbles tickled her nose and she took a long thirsty draught.

It was turning into quite a party, everyone chatting, laughing, forgetting why they were there except for the occasional guilty moment. Andrea avoided thinking about it too as she moved among them, talking, smiling, being the perfect hostess.

But at last, the final hypocritical hug was given, and the last guest departed.

Andrea sighed and locked the door. Then, after checking that the caterers were doing a good job of cleaning up, she poured herself a fifth glass of champagne and took it up to her room.

CHAPTER THREE

Sometime in the very early morning, during that small gap between days when not one car roars along the distant freeway, a ghostlike figure moved swiftly through the ground floor rooms. One by one it collected all the photographs of the dark girl with the haunting eyes. There seemed an inordinate number: on the bookcase, coffee table, end tables, on the grand piano and hung on walls. They were even by the coat rack in the hall and in the kitchen. In some Lesley Clayton was accompanied by a young man, but in most she stood alone, long hair blowing in the wind of some wild, stone-walled land, lips slightly parted as though trying to say something.

Arms filled, the figure went into the yard behind the house and dropped everything, frames and all, with a loud crash into the garbage can. Then she tightly fastened the lid.

A light blinked on upstairs in the guest room where the two sisters slept.

Andrea looked up. Soon those bitches would be gone and Lesley Clayton would be truly dead.

"Mother, what on earth are you doing?"

She turned to see her son framed in the kitchen doorway. Leslie Clayton James. Named after "her". That was the cruelest thing Robert had ever done. But he had been such a beautiful baby. She remembered the inquisitive toddler and then the enquiring little boy. Where were they now? A deep, unexpected sense of loss threatened to overwhelm her and she must have wavered because Leslie sprang down the steps and helped her back inside.

Sitting, elbows on the kitchen table, Andrea fought a confusion of feelings. It must be the champagne…

"Here, Mom, have some coffee. It's been a crappy day what with the funeral and all. You ought to try to sleep."

"I couldn't."

"I know, me neither. You were tough. I knew you wouldn't cry though."

She looked up into his worried young face as he poured tepid liquid into the cup he had set in front of her. "You did?"

He shrugged and turned to fill one for himself. "You never do."

No, she thought, never since you've been old enough to remember. She watched a bubble float and burst. Before that there were too many tears. Had this child of hers never wondered about her feelings toward the woman he was named after? He had just accepted his father's late fiancée as another member of the family, following his mother's example. But of course, how could it have been otherwise?

"It hasn't really sunk in," Leslie was saying, sitting across from her, both hands around his cup, seeking warmth. "Y'know when you phoned about his heart attack I was listening to one of those tapes he used to send instead of writing."

"He did them while he drove to work. He was a busy man."

"He was talking to me while you were telling me he was dead. And when you hung up he was still talking and I kept on listening. He sounded more real than you. I couldn't believe he was gone. I still can't." His voice quavered and he sipped his drink so she couldn't see his eyes.

Surely he wasn't going to break down. She couldn't bear that.

"I'd told him I wanted to join the army if the fighting started. I'll be eighteen soon. He said to wait. 'Stay with Mother, she'll need you,' he said in that last tape. But you don't. You don't need anyone, do you? You're about the toughest person I know."

"It's important to be self sufficient." Andrea reached for a teaspoonful of sugar from the crystal bowl, stirred it briskly into her coffee, then lifted it to her lips. "This tastes terrible," she said.

"What'll you do now?"

"Rinse these and go to bed, I suppose."

"I mean, now Dad's gone?"

"Why should I do anything?"

"I don't know… I just thought…" His eyes, big, green and pleading, met hers. "Dad'll be remembered as someone pretty special, won't he? I didn't realize how important he was 'till I heard it all in church today. We should be really proud of him."

Andrea scarcely heard the words. Those eyes, his father's, had unnerved her, like a memory from long ago and she escaped to the sink and the rush of hot water. She shouted over the noise, "Now you go back to bed. I'll straighten up here."

"Sure you're OK?"

"I'm fine." He needed her to speak to him, console him, she knew that, but she couldn't and he should know better than to expect it of her. She did, however, go over and kiss his cheek, marveling at the bristly feel of it. "By the way, how long are you staying?"

"Should go back tomorrow, exams are coming up."

So short a visit. "Whatever you wish. Goodnight."

He seemed to hesitate, then sighed and left.

Andrea cleared the table and as she emptied her son's barely touched coffee down the drain she noticed that the polish on one of her fingernails was peeling. Damn! She'd had to cancel today's session with her manicurist. She hated having to change plans. Her hair too. She'd never have time to get to her appointment with Enrique and his specially mixed ash-blonde tomorrow with that damn lawyer's meeting at nine.

Always impeccably groomed, hair in a sleek chignon, Andrea had worked hard to project her aura of the perfectly assured, executive's wife who wanted for nothing. Knowing that only Lesley could be beautiful to Robert she had instead concentrated on following the latest fashions, favoring red, and being successful. The community's Volunteer Award had been presented to her so many times it had become embarrassing and finally the trophy was given her name and she was asked to do the presenting. She had also been Woman of the Year more than once and Robert had seemed pleased. The admiration of her peers, and their envy, were further proof of her success, and the fact that she had no close friends was also as it should be— they would have visited and asked questions about all those photos. Everything was habit now. Her image set as in marble. Only strangers, at first meeting, sometimes tried to become familiar, perhaps seeing something in her large grey eyes she hadn't been able to extinguish. But she quickly let them know they had made a mistake. She had been safe for many years now, the woman who could be hurt was long gone.

Andrea washed the two cups and saucers, dried and returned them to their cupboard. Then she opened the dishwasher and, with perverse pleasure, found it full of dirty dishes. She would have been surprised had she not found something left undone by the caterers. It didn't matter how much you paid them. She removed each plate and dish, each glass, and gave it its second rinsing of the evening, then she carefully replaced everything in the washer, inspecting closely for chips as she did so. Soap. On. It sounded exceptionally loud. The kitchen seemed to tremble. Andrea wiped the drain board with deft strokes and looked around. What else could she do to make this night hurry to its end?

CHAPTER FOUR

"What ever are you about?"

"You woke us up!"

The two sisters crowded the kitchen doorway in their baggy, beige, woolen dressing gowns.

Andrea held the dishcloth under the tap and turned the water on hard, as though she would flush the two annoyances away. Not once in all the twenty years they had been paying their dreaded annual visits had they lifted a finger to help her. Those visits during which they had fawned over Robert and Leslie, buying them treats with money she suspected Rob initially provided, and involving them in long discussions about changes in the house and garden while ignoring her. Leslie called them Auntie Agnes and Auntie Effie as they would have been had the girl in the photos lived, because these two carrion crows were Lesley's aunts, had raised her, in fact, so they were part of the deal. Andrea kept out of their way as much as possible, leaving the house early and coming home late.

"All that bashing about, and the dishwasher going, of all things."

"We need sleep even if you don't!" Agnes pouted a leathery upper lip.

"We're all upset about Robert, you know. You mustn't think only of yourself. We'll miss him dreadfully!" Effie whipped out a handkerchief and began to whimper, moving into the comfort of her sister's arm.

"Never mind, Love, he's with "her" now. We should be happy for him. Come on, let's go back to bed." With one last acrimonious glance over her shoulder, Agnes led her sister away.

Andrea's hands twisted the cloth as though strangling it. She had thought she was beyond feeling. Had trained herself so nothing could get through to her. But now… Robert was gone. Damn them! How could those women speak to her like that? But hadn't they always?

She could almost feel the hard wood under her knees and the back of the pew in front digging into her forehead as she did every time she remembered herself praying, quivering with fervor, alone in St. John's church more than twenty years before. "Oh God, please, please make Robert ask me to marry him. I'll die if I lose him. Please, please, I'll do anything! Put up with anything. Just let me spend my life with him. Please!" She had been so passionate then.

Andrea turned out the light and went upstairs to the room she and Robert had shared. She stood in the doorway and automatically listened for his breathing. Nothing. She got into her side of the bed.

For a few moments all was still then, with a rustle of sheets, she again arose and, in the dark, made her way to the dresser. She took the one remaining photo of Lesley Clayton and stood looking at it, needing no light to know every nuance of that beautiful face.

"Excuse me, you dropped this." She remembered being that young college student, twenty years before, holding out a snapshot to the brooding, handsome young man she had watched with yearning since he arrived in class.

"Thanks."

He would have snatched it and gone if Andrea had not held on. "She's beautiful. Who is she?"

"My fiancée. She's dead." He spat it out as though wanting to hurt himself.

"I'm so sorry. She looks special, not like girls here. Would you tell me about her?"

He had looked searchingly into her face, as though judging her sincerity, then asked her out for coffee.

Thus had begun her time of listening as he poured forth the story of his doomed love affair. Swept up in the romance of it she urged him on… and fell hopelessly in love.

Andrea placed the portrait face down. Then she went back to bed and collapsed into a deep sleep.

CHAPTER FIVE

The next few days were crammed with visits to her lawyer, writing letters and honoring her various commitments.

"Honestly, Andrea, let someone else organize the fund drive. Stay home and rest, we'll manage."

"No, no, I'm quite all right, Jane. I'll see you at the meeting tonight at eight." And, as usual, Andrea was too busy to feel anything except a weary triumph at the end of each successfully completed twenty-four hours. The uninformed would never have suspected she was newly bereaved.

Naturally Robert's affairs were in perfect order and the will, besides leaving his wife amply provided for, also left a tidy sum to the two sisters. Andrea noted the smug expressions on their faces when they were told the news; could almost see dry little tongues flick out to lick their lips, but all she could think was that now they would go home forever.

But they didn't—and she couldn't understand why. It wasn't as though they were busy doing anything. They didn't even help prepare meals. Just sat around reading the tabloids and waiting. But for what? Andrea refused to give them the satisfaction of asking or showing that their presence affected her in any way. This was habit. The sisters had always searched for ways to crack her façade. Ways Robert wouldn't notice; small irritations like a mosquito in the dark. She, though always aware, acted oblivious to their efforts. It had been a long silent war and she wasn't going to let them win now.

Five days passed. She asked the lawyer if there was anything else, but no, so far as he knew everything had been accounted for and the sisters understood that their inheritance would be mailed to them in due course. Each day Andrea looked for signs of imminent departure, such as their things being collected from all over the house where they had been scattered for, like cats, the sisters seemed compelled to mark each room. But the tea-stained paperbacked book still straddled the arm of the couch, brown scarves draped the hall stand, galoshes flopped by the front door, a comb with gray hair in it lay on the sideboard by the flowers in the dining room, and a pair of woolen caps, looking like knobs of fungus, decorated the stair rail.

And so Andrea waited and wondered, and afterward thanked whatever angel looked over her for the phone call that kept her home that Thursday afternoon in late March.

It was raining, that light wet rain that slides softly down newly opened throats of spring flowers, and the house smelled of the toast on which Agnes and Effie appeared to exist. As she worked in her office Andrea could hear them chattering in the kitchen. She must attend a meeting at four but it wasn't far and the reporter whose call she awaited had promised to phone by three thirty. It was that now. Damn! Why couldn't people be punctual?

She put on her Burberry and went into the hall to get her umbrella but, as she reached for it, both the doorbell and the telephone rang simultaneously. One of the sister's most infuriating habits was that of rushing to answer any bells that rang, on the pretext of being helpful, but this time with two going at once they had to make a choice. As Andrea continued toward the door she heard the phone being cut off in mid trill.

A heavyset stranger enveloped in an over-large poncho stood on the step. Raindrops clung to his eyebrows and his eyes peered through misty glasses. "Mrs. James?"

"Yes."

"Mr. James."

"I'm sorry, he's not…"

But the man wasn't listening. Instead he was wrestling about under the voluminous folds of his raingear. After a few moments his arms emerged holding a large, gold foil covered box which he thrust toward her. Visions of Christmas and birthday gifts popped into mind but this could be neither, and Andrea stepped back suspecting a mistaken address.

"Mr. James," the man repeated.

Andrea glanced behind him to where a shiny black Cadillac hummed at the curb. "Oh my God!" she said, suddenly comprehending. "Yes. Mr. James. Thank you." She took the box, her arms sagging at the surprising heaviness of it.

"The certificate for travel, in case." He lay an envelop on top.

They smiled politely at one another, and she closed the door.

"Has it come then?" She turned to find the two sisters bearing down on her, eyes fixed on the bulky package in her arms. Agnes' hands were already on it before Andrea realized what was happening. She tightened her grip. "What on earth...! Who called?" It flashed through her mind that they had gone mad, they never had seemed quite normal.

"I told him you were busy. Is that it, Agnes?" The other sister joined them, almost toppling as she leaned toward her goal.

"We'll take it—pack it—right away. Effie—call the airline— perhaps—we can—get a flight—tomorrow." Agnes' words came out in small explosions as she tugged at the box Andrea refused to relinquish.

"Stop!" Andrea jerked it free of Agnes' claws and held it overhead, out of the smaller woman's reach. "Whatever do you think this is? What are you doing?"

Both sisters went suddenly still, Effie half way toward the phone and Agnes with both hands outstretched. Her mouth was tight, mean and wrinkled as she said. "They're Robert's ashes, of course, so you might as well give them to us now."

"I don't understand. Why should I give them to you?"

The sisters glanced at each other. "I don't think she knows."

Andrea caught a note of glee in Agnes' words. "Know what?" she said, steeling herself against whatever was to come.

She could read the signs. The eager, damp eyes, chins pointed toward her from wrinkled necks, fingers curved like talons, and flat chests rising and falling in excited, shallow breaths.

"Robert wrote that after he died we were to take him back to Starwell and scatter him over Lesley's grave."

"Nonsense!" Andrea forced herself to remain impassive but inwardly her heart had gone cold and she knew that, as the coup de grace of Robert's love story, it would be true.

"Get the paper, Effie," trumpeted Agnes.

The two of them waited, listening to Effie scamper upstairs. Quickly she was back triumphantly waving a white document.

Andrea's eyes blurred as she scanned the words in Robert's handwriting, witnessed by the scrawls of Agnes and Effie. In the background Agnes' voice prattled on, explaining how Robert, some years before, had made them promise to give this to Andrea when appropriate, if he wasn't able to tell her first. Andrea stared at the paper seeing only black lines, but she wouldn't look up until she was sure her face showed nothing.

"You must let us carry out his last wish. It's only right his final resting place is with her."

"Yes, you must let us take him back to Lesley," said Effie.

Of course, it didn't matter. It was right. On and on the voices shrilled as Andrea numbly accepted Lesley's final victory. But it didn't have to be a victory for these two harridans who thought they had finally gotten a blow to the quick. Andrea lifted her chin and swallowed hard. "No, I will not."

Her voice had come out firm and quiet and it took a moment for Agnes to pull her face back together. "We'll take this to a lawyer. He'll make you give him to us," she spluttered.

"I think not. I, his wife, not you, will carry out Robert's last request." With that Andrea strode past the two women who gaped like goldfish, pushing them roughly out of her way. At the foot of the stairs she paused. "Effie, continue with that phone call. I want you and your sister out of my house as soon as possible, and I never want to see either of you again. You hear me? Never!"

She stuffed the paper into the pocket of her raincoat and continued up to her bedroom. With the door firmly closed she set the gold box on the glass top of her dressing table and stood looking at it. "How could you do that, Robert? Didn't you think how I might feel? Did God make you do this as my final test?" For a moment she remained motionless, head bowed, shoulders sagging. Then she straightened. But it didn't matter. No one would know, except those two cretins now preparing to leave her life forever. She looked at her watch. She was late for the meeting. To hell with it, there were more important things to be done, like booking a flight to London, writing notes to her various committees explaining the need for a vacation to recuperate from her husband's death, and preparing for her departure.

She called the travel agent from the phone on her nightstand and booked open return tickets for next Friday's flight from San Francisco to Heathrow. Her passport was in the wall safe behind the painting of the ballerina. Thank goodness it was up to date. She thumbed through it. Greece, Italy, France. Each year they had gone someplace but never to England. In the beginning she had been afraid Robert would suggest it, and had lived in terror that if they did go Lesley's long arms would reach from the grave and take him completely away from her. But he never had and she had come to the conclusion that such a trip must be too painful for him to even consider. Sometimes she wondered how he managed to bear the yearly reminder provided by Lesley's two aunts.

Laying her passport aside she fingered Robert's, half thinking he'd need it. Foolishness. She put his back, then looked though her jewelry. Expensive but not much use. Too dangerous to wear these days. What was this wad of papers secured by a large clip? Of course, the papers to the cottage. She'd almost forgotten about the place Robert had bought in Starwell for himself and Lesley to live in after they were married. In the beginning he had often spoken about it. Goodness knows what he'd planned to do for a living! She'd never asked. It was just a wonderfully romantic idea and she had wholeheartedly agreed that he should never sell it nor let anyone else live there.

He sent checks periodically to some caretaker. The sisters were supposed to keep an eye on it although, as they'd moved to a town quite some distance away, Andrea suspected their check-ups were few and far between. She unfolded a piece of paper. The caretaker's name and address. Good, she'd wire and have the place made ready for her. After all, it was hers now. She glanced toward the photo, still face down, and felt a small glow of satisfaction.

A brisk rapping disturbed her thoughts and she opened the door to Agnes. Effie hovered in the hall beyond. "Well?"

"We've a flight tomorrow morning at nine."

"I'm glad to hear it."

"We should leave here by six-thirty. You ought to fill the car with petrol tonight… to be sure, you know."

"It would be too dreadful to get stuck in the middle of the Bay Bridge." This annoying whine of Effie's had followed her sister's reminder about gas every time there had ever been the least hint of them driving in a westerly direction, but today Andrea scarcely noticed.

"You honestly think…?" What was the use, they were what they were. "The cab company's in the yellow pages. I'd phone now if I were you." She shut the door firmly on the gasp of toast breath and finally removed her raincoat.

Before retiring that night, she put Robert into a suitcase. The strongest. There mustn't be any accidents.

Sleep came quickly filled with dreams as confused as a box of puzzle parts. For one wayward second she felt grief for the loss of a hollow-cheeked romantic with burning eyes. But he had left her long ago. An alien tear slipped down the sleeping Andrea's cheek and onto her pillow.

Next morning Agnes and Effie had gone, toast crumbs on the kitchen counter their only traces. Andrea whisked those into the wastebasket and paused, relishing the silence. "Thank God!"

she whispered.

During the intervening six days she sorted Robert's clothes. They could have belonged to a stranger. Finally, packed in boxes, she dragged everything out to the curb to be picked up by a charity organization. After that she planned her own wardrobe, deciding what to take and what to buy. She ordered the cleaning lady to come Wednesday instead of Thursday, and she called a dealer to take Robert's BMW. She made appointments with the people who were to take charge of her various duties and told them what to do. Finally she phoned her son.

"Where'd you say you were going, Mom?"

"To England. Yorkshire probably." No need to tell him about the ashes.

"D'you think you should?"

Andrea couldn't speak.

"Mother?"

"Leslie, why should I not go there?"

"I only thought… Okay, Mom, if you think it's all right. When're you coming back?"

Did her own son think it wrong of her to step on Lesley's hallowed ground? Andrea sighed and was tempted to hang up. Instead she said, "I don't know. I'll write. Goodbye." She rested her forehead on her hand. So damn tired of it all. For a few minutes she stayed there by the phone then she straightened and went to the drawer where the photo albums were kept. She took out the largest and opened it, from the back first. There was Leslie after the end of term ceremonies last summer, grinning from ear to ear, his father's arm draped across his shoulders. She had been holding the camera, she never had pictures taken of herself. She looked back through photos of her son's school years and missed him, although he'd seldom been home. His father, who often stood beside the boy, she ignored, but when the album opened prior to her son's grade school days, showing him accompanied by a tall dark young

Robert she shivered and snapped the book shut. She looked again to the end where her husband was a heavily jowled, potbellied man, pompous with importance. She sat looking at him for a long time. He is the one in the box upstairs, not the other. Remember that, Andrea, remember.

On the morning of her departure, at the very last moment and scarcely noticing she did it, she slipped the one remaining photo of the dark eyed girl into the bottom of her suitcase. She didn't know why, she'd meant to throw it away like the others.

CHAPTER SIX

Flying has certainly lost its glamour, Andrea thought as she pushed through San Francisco airport's milling hordes of casually, often scruffily, dressed adults and their wailing children. She wondered if the number of young men in uniform was a sign that rumors of war might soon become a reality. There were more police too.

Unintelligible announcements came over the public address system and mixed with the hum of voices and roar of departing aircraft. Warm air suddenly became stifling, and sucked the moisture from her skin. Andrea drew her coat back from the chocolaty fingers of a small boy who reached out to her, and circumnavigated countless islands of people with their bags and suitcases, skis, knapsacks and boxes. When her way was blocked by an elderly man pushing a white haired woman in a wheelchair, she impatiently wondered why such people travelled at all, just being a nuisance to everyone. At that moment the woman raised a hand, reaching back to pat her husband's and, as he smiled down at her, Andrea, missing her chance to pass, felt a touch of envy. At least she and Robert had never argued, never had one fight in all those years. Yet they could never have ended up like that old couple. It would have been nice though...

"We need to x-ray your handbag, Ma'am."

Andrea plunked her bag on the belt then went back and forth through the security gate several times before discovering it was her scarf clasp that was setting off the alarm.

Her heels tapped on the shiny floor as she walked to the

door of the VIP lounge. Inside it was hushed and dark, with soft music, and she sank gratefully onto a couch. God! What a week! She ordered Scotch with a splash of water, thinking it might quench the guilt that lingered from watching the blue end of Robert's case tip up and disappear down the conveyer belt with the other luggage; quite a comedown from his usual first class. Well, she certainly couldn't carry him on with her, and the box was well padded in newspapers. The idea of his last remains resting among her undies hadn't seemed right so now she had two cases to struggle through England with.

She took her reading glasses from her handbag and put them on, then retrieved a brown notebook with Executive Time Organizer engraved on the cover. Opening it, she obtained a sense of comfort from the neat notes precisely detailing her actions for the next forty-eight hours. At least for that much longer she was in control; and having control was very important to Andrea James.

"Are you staying in London?"

She looked up, irritated. A young woman had plunked down in the adjacent seat and, as Andrea turned to look, her glasses slid to perch on the pinched tip of her nose, magnifying orange lipstick that clashed with an expensive maroon sweater. Round blue eyes eagerly awaited an answer.

"No," said Andrea sharply, pushing her glasses up and turning back to her notebook.

"I am. I'm going to live there." The voice sounded horribly cheerful. "I'm getting married Sunday. Wanted to do it fast. According to the papers anything could happen. Russia in turmoil, the Middle East. Something could erupt any minute and we'd never get together. I mean, I was getting real scared."

Andrea grunted and kept her eyes on her notes.

"He's my girlfriend's cousin. I met him when he visited her a couple of summers ago. Isn't it weird how things work out? Who'd ever believe we'd even meet each other, me in California, him in London."

She paused a moment, then seemingly undeterred by

Andrea's obvious lack of interest, continued to babble. "Neither of us has dated anyone else since we met."

Andrea sighed, removed her glasses, then snapped them and her notebook back into her bag. She turned to the girl. "How do you know?"

"Know? Know what?"

Oh the foolish innocence in those shining eyes! Someone should tell her about that awful lipstick. What effect would it have on the young man waiting in London? Maybe he was used to it, amazing what one could get used to. "Know he hasn't cheated. More than likely he has." It felt good to say that. The stupid girl had no right to be so cheerful, interrupting people who wanted to be left alone.

But the words seemed not to dampen the silly creature's spirits at all, in fact a grin twitched and tugged the girl's mouth toward her ears. "I know because he told me!"

Silly, silly little bitch. "Humph," was all Andrea said, swirling amber liquid around her glass.

"Don't you believe in trust? A lot of people don't, but I do. You see if he can trust me, which I know he can, then I can trust him. Now if I ever deceived him then I couldn't trust anyone, could I? But, as it is, I can." With a satisfied shrug the girl took out a paperback. "Dick Francis. I always read him when I fly. Toby, that's my fiancé, does too. Do you like him?"

"No."

"That's too bad. Which have you read?"

"I haven't." Oh why didn't the silly girl shut up with her youth and foolish dreams and hopes for a perfect future!

"Haven't? You mean you haven't read any? Then how do you know you don't like him?"

"I know." Because you do and you are so different from me, Andrea thought, and you are so stupid.

At that moment the announcement for their flight to commence boarding came over the intercom and Andrea promptly finished her drink, stood up, flung the scarf attached to her fawn cashmere coat over her shoulder, and strode toward the door. She ignored the, "Goodbye, it was nice talking to you," until she had almost left the room, then she paused and looked back to where the girl still struggled with a coat and two boxes. "Was I ever that young?" she thought.

"This way, Mrs. James," said a smiling attendant, and Andrea was escorted to the gate and up the ramp onto the 747.

Ensconced in her first class seat, Andrea could do nothing but relax for the next eleven hours. As the plane flew over San Francisco, she looked down at the clustered high-rises pointing upward from their shining, almost island—and there was the slender orange bridge carrying traffic to and from Marin. All so familiar. Home. Where was she going? What would she find? She reached into her handbag for her time organizer. 10:00 AM arrival. 10:15 customs. 10:30 shuttle to hotel. 11:05 bath. 11:30 nap. (Put do not disturb sign on door). Set alarm for 4:30. 4:45 walk.

Andrea read to the end of the day with 'lights out at 8PM.' then with a satisfied sigh put the book away.

"Scotch, please," she said to the questioning flight attendant and soon settled back with it and a Town and Country magazine. The engines throbbed. She could hear dinner being organized in the galley. She was nowhere at all.

After a while she slept, awoke to pick at her meal, then slept again. Once she walked to the rear toilet to stretch her legs and passed the girl from the lounge in animated conversation with another young woman. Foolish youth, they didn't know. She looked so happy. Quite pretty really.

Ignoring the movie Andrea slept most of the night and awoke aching and longing for a cup of coffee. When she had it in her hand she raised the window shade and looked out. Sunrise brightened a thread of white water that married sea to land far below and her stomach gave an involuntary lurch of excitement. England! How she had longed to come here before she met Robert, her imagination fed by all those books she had read as an only child. Wuthering Heights and the Bible had gone with her to college as family photos accompanied other homesick freshmen, and how often she had imagined herself to be Cathy looking for Heathcliff among all those callow college boys. Then she had found him in the dark-eyed, grieving Robert but he had already found, and lost, his Cathy. Andrea recognized her as soon as she saw Lesley's photograph. It had been like a miracle.

Below checkered fields in shades of green took the place of ocean and the plane's shadow darted over farms and villages. Andrea rested her forehead against the window. Was she really here just to complete the pact she had made so long ago for Robert, or was it to confront Lesley's ghost face to face? She should have stayed home doing all the things her substitutes were sure to be making a mess of. A toy car drove along a pencil line below and Andrea envied the driver for being safe in a world to which he belonged. The empty pages in her note book loomed like the precipice she would have to face tomorrow. She could barely remember a time when she hadn't known exactly what she would be doing the next day—and the next week. In fact she'd once heard her son joke that his mother was like a well programmed computer. But what happened to a computer when it had no program?

Ping. The seat belt sign went on. Coffee cups were collected and the engines seemed to stop, leaving a hollow emptiness—a floating sensation after the solid roar that had powered them through the flight. Andrea fixed her hair and makeup then rested her head against the back of the seat, eyes shut. Thump. That was the wheels being lowered. Now began the long descent. Andrea went deaf.

Bump—bump. They sped along the runway and dragged to a halt. Voices sounded muffled and distant. Someone handed Andrea's coat down from the overhead compartment.

It was a long walk from the plane, and through the surrounding glass she could see cars gliding along wet pavement below. When finally she reached Immigration she was wished a pleasant vacation and sent on to find a cart and collect her luggage for Customs. Somehow she had expected porters here.

"And what might this be?" The custom's officer had removed Robert's box from its colorful nest of San Francisco's Sunday Examiner.

"Ashes." Andrea answered testily. She was tired and the air, unbearably warm and dry, made her desperate to get outside. Besides, she had a schedule to keep, an obligation to her late husband who, although he had placed no time limit on his return, at least from what she had seen on her quick glance, must surely have wanted it to be speedy.

"Ashes?" the man repeated, shaking the box and looking at her as though his eyes would read some hidden truth. "Sorry, Madam, but I'll have to take a look."

Andrea's hand shot out in Robert's defense. "I have a certificate. For Christ's sake you can't open it! Can't have my husband blowing around your airport!" The thought flashed that maybe that was just what should happen, then she could turn around and go home where she belonged. Perspiration trickled between her breasts.

"Umm." The man, still watching her, called a colleague and the two conferred while Andrea fumed. Couldn't they see the kind of person she was? How dare they suspect her! This wouldn't happen if Robert were here—all of him, that is.

Most of the people from her plane had left, the last ones eyeing her with curiosity. The girl in the maroon sweater waved but Andrea pretended not to notice.

"We'll have to x-ray it, I'm afraid. Shan't be long."

Alone in the empty room Andrea took out the address of her hotel and studied it so anyone watching would think her unconcerned, but inwardly she seethed and blamed her late husband. Suddenly her ears popped and her senses were inundated by airport sounds. She didn't like Robert being out of her sight like this. What were they doing with him? Ah, at last … "You were long enough," she snapped, snatching the box from the customs officer's hands and holding it against her for a moment before lowering it back among the gaudy wrappings.

"Sorry for the delay, Mrs. James, but we must be certain, you know."

"Do I look like a smuggler?" Andrea asked. "I 'd think some of those other people were a damn sight more likely."

"Smugglers come in all shapes and sizes, Madam, and so do terrorists. You'd be surprised. It's my job to be suspicious. I don't mean to offend, but you haven't the appearance of someone carrying her late husband's ashes. I must say we don't get a lot, but those we do have a certain mourning look about them."

As Andrea closed the lid of the case it occurred to her that perhaps she shouldn't have packed Robert in the Sunday comics. It was just that they were convenient and her mind had been so full of other things...

What a pain it was travelling alone. Oh well, better get on with it. So awkward heaving bags about. Damn, there was a smudge on her coat. The hotel would have a cleaners.

As she boarded the minibus waiting to transport passengers to the nearby hotel where she had reserved a room she looked down into a small car easing past and recognized the maroon sweater. The girl's head was turned away but she could see the driver's hand tightly grasping hers. He was wearing a maroon sweater too.

CHAPTER SEVEN

The hotel was satisfactory and, after she verified that her rental car would indeed be at the door by eight the next morning, Andrea entered the elevator pleased to note she was on schedule despite the holdup at customs.

Andrea followed her itinerary to the letter so her only experience of England that first day was a short walk through drizzle to a newsstand. There she bought postcards to send to people back home, reminding them of their responsibilities, and two bigger cards for her son.

After ordering soup and salad back at the hotel she looked around at the other diners; East Indians, Asians and Africans identified by appearance, French and Germans by the accents she could hear mixed in with the communal buzz. Where were the English? Of course the guests were all tourists, like she was. But she wasn't a tourist, she was here on business, a job she would complete as soon as possible then fly back into the comfort of responsibility. Ah yes, she thought as steam rose from the bowl being slipped under her nose, she would be heading back home in no time.

In her room a small lamp glowed beside the bed which had been remade and turned down. Sleep would be good tonight. But as Andrea reached to put her handbag on the dressing table her breath caught in her throat and her eyes locked on the familiar gaze of the dark eyed girl in the photo now propped against the mirror. She stood frozen—then reason asserted itself. Of course, the photo must have fallen from her suitcase and the maid had, quite naturally, picked it up. Why on earth had she brought it to begin with? She didn't remember having put it in. Robert was the one for photos. Hadn't he placed those large, framed portraits of Lesley all over their home, even on the wall overlooking their king-sized bed? Or had she done it knowing it would please him? She really couldn't remember, but surely in the beginning that wild ex-fiancée had been more a figment of her imagination than reality—more a symbol of Andrea's own romantic free spirit. Like the child who had been her imaginary friend before she'd learned to read.

When had Lesley's smile begun to mock and the eyes that had seemed so hauntingly beautiful to the young college girl begun to flash triumph at the new wife? God, it had been awful. "You betrayed that girl," Andrea whispered to the portrait. "You were everywhere. You almost broke that poor kid's heart." There in that British hotel room it was like looking back on someone else. "But you didn't win, Lesley." Andrea's voice choked. "That young wife learned to ignore you, trained herself not to see you until those could have been empty frames on the walls. But she knew enough never to allow any photos to be taken of herself lest Robert compare. You turned that girl into who I am now, Lesley Clayton."

The eyes stared back, quietly waiting, while reflections in the glass camouflaged the look of derision Andrea knew must be there. "All right, damn you, you'll get your ashes, but only because I'm strong enough to stick to my bargain. If you were so almighty powerful why did you die?"

The telephone buzzed. Andrea's elbow jerked and knocked an ashtray to the floor. Three rings later she lifted the receiver.

"You asked for a wake up call, Mrs. James. Could you please affirm the time?" A woman's English voice purred along the line and Andrea had to shake the impression it was Lesley speaking.

She reached to turn on the larger lamp nearby. "Oh. Yes. Seven o'clock please."

"Have a good night, Mrs. James." Click.

Andrea turned back to the photograph but Lesley looked

insignificant now and she slipped the photo back beneath the clothes in her suitcase and snapped the locks.

The Ford Escort arrived promptly at eight and, with her credit card allowing an open date for the car's return, Andrea was on the road by eight-fifteen, following explicit directions to M-1, the highway that would take her straight to the North country. It began to rain. Water from some unknown source dripped steadily onto her left ankle and for a moment she longed for her own solid Acura and the familiar freeways of California. Then, remembering Robert behind her in the trunk, she thought how it wouldn't be long before she would leave him behind and head for home alone. A small voice in her head whispered, "You don't really have to do it. Who'd ever know?"

Andrea's foot stamped down on the accelerator. "I'd know," she blurted, and roared away from the truck that had been preparing to pass her.

She turned on the radio and only caught glimpses of the misty fields and hedges that flashed by on her left. Now and then she'd see the rain-smudged ghost of a church steeple and clustered roofs of a village but it all seemed unreal.

After the road forked at Northhampton, traffic was lighter and she relaxed, easing back to seventy. She had been driving for two hours and with relief pulled off at an island with a restaurant called the Little Chef. Looking at her map Andrea was astonished to find she had already covered over half her journey. England was small. A spasm of unease swept through her. She had expected to take all day to reach Starwell. Another couple of hours at the most and she'd be there! She wasn't ready.

"Coffee, Luv?"

"Yes, please. Black." How odd to be called Luv. Some people must like it. Especially when they're alone and cold. "And I'll have a scone too, please." Not that she was hungry, she just needed some time in this steamy, bacon and coffee atmosphere. She glanced through a newspaper left by a previous customer. America on the Verge. More Sanctions. Fighting in another country she'd never before heard of. Britons Cringe at Higher Taxes. All the same stomach-churning stuff. She had a second coffee and a third, then studied the map. Once her hand strayed into her handbag searching for her Time Organizer but quickly came out empty. There were only vacant pages there now.

"Fill it up again, Luv?"

"Oh. No thanks."

"'Ere's yer check then."

No more excuses. She looked through the speckled window pane at a gray world that made her think of the twilight zone. One more small procrastination—a visit to the restroom—then she left warmth and safety for rain and traffic, drip still dripping, wipers rhythmically slapping.

Click-clack, click-clack, Les-ley Clay-ton, Les-ley Clay-ton, Les-, over and over again, and the more she tried to stop it the more the name repeated itself. Ah, the radio! Andrea stabbed it on with her forefinger, turning music and voices up loud until at last Lesley was drowned out. In her place was Joan Barker asking for an old Beatle's classic to be played for her boyfriend George. To the beat of A Yellow Submarine the miles hummed under the Escort's wheels and Andrea's spirits lifted. Song followed song. Then the news and more music.

The road split and she left the M1, heading West.

BRADFORD NEXT EXIT.

Andrea sucked in her breath. Surely not so soon! Rain fell harder making it half dark already. Not far to Starwell now! Another hour perhaps. Her top lip became damp. Why not spend the night somewhere first? Arrive fresh at the cottage. Who knew what state it was in. Much better to arrive rested and with a full day ahead of her. That villager, Simpson, who supposedly acted as caretaker... what did Robert know about him except that the Postal Orders he sent were accepted? Yes, tomorrow would be much better.

Andrea exited the motorway and entered congested, rain

slick streets not sure where she was headed.

The sign of the Blue Boar was a godsend and she wrenched the little car out of the traffic's current and into an alley which led to a small courtyard. With an enormous sense of relief she parked and swore nothing would make her drive one foot farther that night.

Rain had slowed to drizzle. She opened the trunk and took out one suitcase, then stayed looking at the other. Was it all right to leave Robert alone? Of course. Carefully she closed the lid but guilt accompanied her all the way to the back entrance of the grey stone Inn. Shut off from the city, everything here was shrouded in quiet and she paused at the door to listen for signs of life. Then, with an impatient shrug, she turned the brass knob and stepped inside.

CHAPTER EIGHT

The heavy door opened grudgingly, scraping across stone. Smells of stale beer tightened Andrea's nostrils as she followed the sound of slopping water up a dark hallway and into a bar. There she was met by a broad blue and white flowered backside seemingly supported by a pair of Wellington boots. Burly arms pumped back and forth working a mop that hurled soapy water over the floor and Andrea watched, fascinated, until the figure jerked upright, pushed a strand of hair off its forehead with the back of one wrist then turned to squint at her through blue marble eyes. A clock struck with sharp, startling strokes. Only four? Andrea glanced in its direction.

"Well?" The woman didn't look as though she had spoken but there was no one else.

Andrea adjusted the strap on her handbag. "I want a room. I presume you have one?"

"Mebbe."

"This is an Inn, isn't it?"

"Aye, and you mun be American."

"I am and I've just driven up from London and am badly in need of a bed if you don't mind."

"Nay, Lass. Don't climb on yer high horse. You Americans allus expect everything to be there right when you want it." She wiped a hand under her nose. "Yer lucky tonight, though, I do 'ave a room ready. Follow me." She lumbered off through a door at the other end of the bar.

Andrea followed into an unlit hallway, warm and rich with smells which must have been permeating the dark walls for hundreds of years. The woman had disappeared through a swinging partition up ahead. Andrea stopped, left but not alone. Instead she had never felt more jostled by humanity. She found herself straining to hear the voices she knew must be just out of her wavelength. This hall was alive, as though each customer had left part of himself as he passed through. Andrea wondered if part of herself was now also embedded here. And then she wondered what foolishness had come over her in that dark space and pushed her way out.

"There!" A light clicked on over a counter illuminating the woman she had followed and who now wore a purple felt hat and luminescent pink lipstick. "Well, Miss. So you want a room? I have a single, overlooking the street but you say you're tired so I expect a little noise won't bother you. Just sign here will you."

Andrea, who would have taken anything, signed without question. Then the woman clicked off the light and Andrea again waited in darkness. She heard the motion of the swinging door, then felt the woman push past her. "Follow me. Some folks complain it's too dark for 'em but we don't turn on lights 'til daylight's gone. Conserving energy you know. Patriotic and all."

Andrea wondered how dark it did get if this was considered daylight, but her eyes grew accustomed to it as she climbed stairs behind the woman's broad back and followed her along a slanting passageway.

"That's the bath," the woman muttered, banging her fist on a door as she passed, eliciting a shout from behind it. "And here's your room."

This was two rooms farther on and as the door swung open Andrea caught a pleasant whiff of furniture polish, lavender and a hint of the ubiquitous stale beer. Daylight, although dim, allowed her to see a single bed, an oak dresser with brass handles, a tipsy looking chair and a rail with a drape which presumably hid some hangers behind it. A mullioned window, with maroon curtains on either side, was set about knee high above the sloping dark oak floor, and from outside came the swish of passing traffic.

The woman stood as though daring her guest to utter the mildest complaint at which she would be only too happy to usher her back out into the rain, but when she realized no negative reaction was forthcoming she relaxed and became more approachable.

"Is there someplace where I can eat later?" Andrea asked, putting down her suitcase and rubbing feeling back into the hand which had held it.

"Aye, you'll find summat down the road apiece, and if you don't want to go out we 'ave Shepherd's pie tonight, or bangers and mash." The woman almost smiled. "It's right cozy downstairs on a night like this."

Rain dashed against the window as if on cue. "I'll probably do that then. Thank you."

"You 'ave a nice rest then." The woman nodded her purple hat and left, closing the door which immediately swung back open. Andrea heard her heavy footsteps proceed a short distance then pause. Thump, thump. A man's voice gargled angrily from inside the bathroom. The footsteps continued on.

Andrea smiled, then shut the door and slid the latch. Having no key made her a little nervous, but after a moment's hesitation she shrugged and went to the window. The street with its flood of cars and jostling umbrellas was like a scene from a movie. All those lives… everyone rushing toward whatever the evening held while she waited in limbo. Sleepy limbo. She turned to the bed. A soak would be wonderful but not in that bathroom. She undressed to her slip and got under the covers.

The hum of voices pulsed against her floor from the pub below. An exceptionally loud burst of laughter had awakened her and Andrea lay listening. It was really dark now. She had no idea what the time was nor how long she'd slept. It was very tempting to stay wrapped in this chrysalis of sleep, but no, if she didn't get up she'd awake starving in the middle of the night.

She unpacked her navy blue wool dress, pearl necklace and

earrings, and by the time she was ready, having redone her makeup in her own folding mirror, she felt prepared to face anything the Blue Boar might present.

Noise and smoke hit her like a wall. Luckily most of the customers were packed around the bar and she was able to find a chair at a small table in a far corner. Her order for whiskey and Shepherd's pie was promptly taken by a young woman with startling blue eye shadow, and the drink arrived quickly, warming her stomach for the steaming meal. Andrea had eaten more than half, and felt like her usual confident self again, before she transferred her attention to the crowd. Fingering her pearls she immediately condemned everyone for looking shabby and smoking too much. A rumble of unintelligible words whirled around her, punctuated by the thud of the darts, and soon she relaxed, floating on tides of laughter and the ebb and flow of voices.

"Mind if I sit here? There seems no place else."

Andrea grudgingly relinquished her sense of invisibility. "Of course," she answered.

If it weren't for the deepness of his voice, she would have thought the man across from her was only a boy, his build was so slight, but his weather beaten face proved him to be much older. She watched amused as he drank thirstily from his mug of beer and she noticed that, although he looked clean, the cuffs of his sports coat were frayed. A change in air currents informed her nose that he wasted no money on deodorants.

"From America, are you?" He wiped foam from his lips and surveyed her with interest. "Tourist or business?"

How did they always know? Andrea was beginning to think she must have US branded on her forehead and it annoyed her. But then maybe this fellow could give her some information. "Business. In a village called Starwell. D'you know it, by any chance?"

"Aye, might say as I do. Can't imagine having business there though. Strange sort of place. Lot of stories."

Andrea leaned forward. "What kind of stories?"

"Just tales to drum up the tourist trade probably. A strange death or two. Now they talk about a ghost shepherd who walks the fells at night. Farmers swear they've had many a sheep saved by him." He drained his glass and laughed. "Course I don't give no side to that sort of yarn but strangers do like to hear it. Look at you."

Andrea quickly leaned back. "You said you'd been there...?"

"Aye, just a couple of times. Can I get you another drink?"

"Let me buy you one."

"Is that what they do in America?"

"What?"

"Women buy drinks for men? I have my own brass, thank you." He stood up and at that moment a voice called from the crush near the bar. "Roger!" Andrea's tablemate waved back. "Colleagues," he said. "I'll be off then." He nodded and left her.

Andrea watched him go, amused and slightly disappointed. She'd have liked to have heard more about Starwell. At least he'd made it real. Sometimes she'd almost begun to doubt if the place existed. Come to think of it Robert used to tell her ghost stories on rainy nights long ago as they cuddled in front of a fire. This country was probably awash in superstition. Andrea caught the eye of the waitress and ordered another drink. Someone turned the extra chair around to join friends at the next table. Again she was alone in the hubbub, sipping from her fresh glass. Tranquility crept over her as she was again submerged in voices. Occasionally she caught a glimpse of the man called Roger, always surrounded by people, usually listening intently, sometimes talking. She wondered what they spoke about.

Time to leave. Tomorrow she must seek out her own ghosts.

It was doubly hard getting to the door this time. As she reached it she heard one male voice above all the chatter. "Well, Doc, there goes that rich American who wanted to buy you a pint."

Andrea paused in the open doorway.

A female voice laughed, "Too bad she's so long in the tooth."

"Nay, I don't think she's as old as she looks. Just too full of her own importance, I think." That was Roger.

"Wouldn't catch me turning down free drinks…"

"Noisy lot those doctors from St. Giles." The proprietress, still in her purple hat and strenuously applied lipstick, had arrived, and like a great ship pushed Andrea out ahead of her. "Sometimes I think they're as barmy as their patients," she sniffed.

"They're doctors in a mental hospital?"

"Aye, ye'd never guess it, would you?"

The door swung to behind them and the woman sailed on leaving Andrea alone. Old? Was forty old? Come to think of it she hadn't felt young for a very long time—but what did it matter anyway.

Upstairs she went straight to the bathroom and pushed open the door only to be met with a loud, "Eh, get out. Wot cher doin'? 'Aven't you learned to knock?"

Andrea sighed as she stared at the man in the tub. It was almost as though she would have been surprised had someone not been there. "You might have turned the lock," she snapped.

With a great surge he stood up and she pivoted on her heel and left, indignant and hoping no one else heard his laughter. Ill mannered idiots these Yorkshire dolts! She slammed her door which rebounded, needing to be closed again more gently.

Andrea stood in the center of the room staring at the closed window curtain. She thought of Robert out there in the car and couldn't remember locking the trunk. Oh Lord, what if someone stole him. Such a tempting package. But she couldn't go outside now, so late and in the rain… with that naked fool running around the passageway. What a nuisance this whole damn thing was, and now she had to wait until the bathroom was empty.

Did she really look old?

CHAPTER NINE

Early morning traffic roared and clattered along the street beside the Blue Boar as Andrea lay in bed planning the day ahead. It was good she'd stopped off for the night; had taken time to prepare a schedule. It put her in control again. Seven o'clock. "Up and at 'em!" She could hear Robert shouting it. That was a very long time ago... hadn't thought of it for ages.

It was her habit to shower first but not today; trooping down the corridor to that bathroom in her robe was unthinkable. Besides she couldn't recall seeing a shower anywhere near that huge tub that took up half the room. Robert would have laughed about the man in there last night—and he would have checked whether all was clear this morning. Never mind, next week she'd be safe home with all her own things around her. Her thoughts rambled as she added an extra dab of deodorant, dressed in chocolate slacks and a tan turtleneck, then looped a silk scarf around her neck. She added a gold chain and earrings, carefully arranged her hair and put on lipstick. Knee high stockings and shoes went on last. One appraising look in the mirror, then she firmly approached the bathroom and was relieved to find the door wide open.

Twenty minutes later Andrea stood in the Inn's empty office and tapped the bell on the counter. The large woman appeared, adjusting her purple hat, and three times questioned her guest's refusal of the breakfast that came with the night's lodging then, shaking her head, she made out the bill. With a sudden sense of urgency, Andrea cut short her chatter, paid, and hurried out into the courtyard and across the cobbles to the car. She opened the

43

trunk and sighed with relief, Robert's case was still there; gold box glowing in its comic strip bed. "Good, you're safe. I hope you had a peaceful night, Robert," she murmured.

Andrea loaded her own luggage and was soon driving through the heart of Bradford with its diesel fumes and confusion of one way streets. But she had studied the map and it wasn't long before she escaped the urban hubbub for a world of narrow lanes and stone walls lightly wrapped in morning mist. The previous day's apprehension had vanished with the rain and now she looked about her with a growing sense of familiarity. It was all so similar to what she had imagined. Grey stone walls crisscrossed the brilliant green dale like sudsy streams running down hillsides to border the road and pool into villages and farms. As the sun did its final unveiling Andrea stopped in a gateway and got out to gaze at the magnificent sweeping distance. She wanted to exclaim to someone how splendid it was and how in some way she felt as though she had come home. She sniffed the clean, sharp, sweet-smelling air as though it were wine and she tipped her head to better hear wind-borne bleating from white dots on the faraway hillsides. It was like revisiting a dream and she stood, lips parted, lost in distance and time.

The rattle of a passing van brought her back. What on earth was she doing! She had groceries to buy and brunch to eat at what, according to the map, looked like the last decent sized town before her destination, and after that... well, the sooner the better.

The winding roads took longer than expected, and once she had to wait while a flock of sheep flooded around her car, stranding her in a sea of wool and wild topaz eyes. A tongue-lolling, black and white Border collie brought up the rear, accompanied by a wiry little man in a dirty raincoat who touched his cap and muttered, " 'Mornin', Mum."

She watched until they were out of sight before starting up again, and a few miles later she roared around the last bend before Farrington.

The town had a cobbled square where she parked and, after carefully locking up, climbed the steep street lined with small shops to arrive out of breath at the grocery store. She noticed how drably the few other women customers were dressed and pitied them for their lack of style and clumsy makeup. They obviously neglected their figures too. Health clubs were probably non-existent here, not that she could talk, she'd joined one but had never found time to go. She did wear good undergarments though so any unwanted flesh was kept under control and hidden beneath her expensive clothes. 'They look downright motherly,' Andrea thought as she selected a loaf of bread. 'At least Leslie could never accuse me of that!'

She purchased the necessary staples plus a string bag to put them in, then found a postcard for her son... a picture of a cottage with moorland rising into blue distance behind it. Faws House was the title below.

She scribbled a note while drinking a bowl of soup in a small cafe with neat white table cloths and lace curtains, and mailed it, with no return address, from the nearby excuse for a post office. America seemed another world seen dimly through the wrong end of a telescope.

Time to get to that village she had never expected to see; the source of all those dreams that had disintegrated into a nightmare. As Andrea walked back downhill the wind caught her scarf and, before she could react, whisked it from her neck into the gutter where it was swept away entangled in the current of recent rain. "Damn!" she muttered, and as she watched that colorful piece of expensive silk disappear she blamed the wind of vindictively trying to make her drab like the locals. Yanking the lapels of her coat close, she tightened her mouth to an angry line, and hurried on.

When she reached the Escort she sat for a moment behind her steering wheel, then jabbed the key into the ignition, started the engine and drove off, leaving a small puff of smoke hovering in the parking lot.

The roads were even narrower now and she could only see

beyond the walls through the rails of periodic gates. She was travelling up a valley, following the curves of the river she saw flashes of to her left. What traffic she met passed without a care but Andrea expected to be sideswiped at any moment and her knuckles only regained color when, after five miles, the road opened upon a cluster of buildings. This must be Starwell. Her stomach coiled into a knot. Intuitively she turned up a lane to her right and as she looked from side to side she could hear Robert's voice, long ago as they had sat on that college bench which seemed a magnet for Berkeley's coldest winds.

"The cottages are stone, built right on the street so it's like passing through a tunnel of windows, and your footsteps echo when you walk to the pub or the dinky post office on the corner."

Andrea had hunched forward listening entranced as her lover extolled the home of his adored fiancée.

"After that first block every house has its own garden crammed with flowers, and right in the middle of the village there's a farm. They drive the cows down the street to be milked there, then back out to the river meadow after. I'd often meet them. Shuffling and lowing. It was kinda nice…"

"I bet Lesley knew them well seeing as she lived there for so long." He had such beautiful dark eyes—and his voice filled her with dreams… she'd give anything to live in a village like that… be loved like Lesley

"Oh, lord yes. She'd just talk kind of softly, say their names, and they'd stop and let her scratch their heads."

Andrea met no cows but as she passed the cottages she wondered which had been the home of the two sisters as they raised Lesley. After the accident the two women had moved to a town some twenty miles away—to escape the memories— they said, although memories certainly hadn't deterred them from visiting Robert once a year. Had he paid their fares? Funny, she'd never thought about how they'd afforded it.

She jolted to a stop and blew her horn at a tractor that pulled out in front of her, but the diminutive, ancient driver ignored her and chugged stubbornly up the road keeping her to a slow crawl behind the border collie that trotted close to his wheels. Glancing into the yard they'd come out of Andrea saw a man pitching hay from a high stack of bales while several calves jostled greedily below. Then the gate slammed shut, ridden to its conclusion by a child who looked a miniature version of the tractor driver.

The cottages were farther apart now and there were several stone barns, back from the road, that looked as though they may have been transformed into houses. The tractor veered out of her way onto a rough lane. The dog glanced back and raised its upper lip in a grin, then Andrea was alone. Ahead was the familiar small, arched, stone bridge Robert had so often mentioned.

At the highest point a woman leaned against the side watching the stream that roared underneath with Springtime ferocity. Seemingly unaware of the approaching Escort until it was alongside she turned, and Andrea found herself looking into a pair of startled grey eyes, strangely light and nakedly direct. Inadvertently Andrea's foot pressed the accelerator and the car spurted forward. When she glanced back the bridge was empty. She stopped and looked more carefully. Nothing. Why did she feel as though she'd seen a ghost? She licked suddenly-dry lips, called herself a fool and drove on, only to brake again in about a hundred yards when she recognized the overgrown driveway on her left, and the iron gate and wall Robert had described so well. She'd almost missed it behind all that fresh foliage. Hard to believe so little had changed in all these years.

Sudden rain lashed through sunshine and a car blew its horn behind her. Quickly she pulled over. The gate looked solidly closed. Damn! Why hadn't the caretaker opened it for her, she'd sent the telegram a week ago. Now the rain was pounding down and she'd have to get soaked. Where had the clouds come from? Andrea draped her raincoat over her head and ran, only to find her entrance barred by chain and padlock. She tugged with slippery fingers thinking how she'd give that blasted caretaker something to think about when she saw him! The coat slid onto her shoulders so rain beat on her head. Suddenly the gate gave, not in the middle but at the left side where it had broken loose from its hinges. Andrea pushed, lifted and dragged until there was room for her car, then ran back and drove through.

CHAPTER TEN

She revved down the short length of gravel driveway and jerked to a stop in front of a white door. The two-storied stone cottage seemed to be asleep in the midst of its rampant, untended garden and as Andrea turned off the engine she could swear she'd seen this same house just recently. Even the fox-head doorknocker was uncannily familiar. Silence but for the light patter of rain. The grass, which had once been lawn, was long and tangled with buttercups and daffodils. A mist of bluebells drifted under trees.

Andrea frowned thinking of her manicured garden in California. It would not take long to get this place fixed up. She'd hire someone from the village to prune branches, tear out weeds and mow the grass. Rip that ivy off the walls too, let some light in and get rid of those wild roses she could see untrimmed toward the back. Maybe pave the drive. Yes, she'd get the place respectable in no time and probably sell it for a decent price. She glanced uneasily behind her toward the car's trunk. No, Robert, this is no longer any of your business.

The rain stopped as abruptly as it had started. Almost as though it poured on purpose to get me wet, Andrea thought, shifting her soggy shoulders. She got out of the car, right into a puddle. "Damn and blast it!"

A bird trilled merrily.

Unexpectedly the front door opened to her touch. She paused to notice 1655 carved on the lintel then ducked under a hanging pot of red geraniums and entered the hallway. A sunbeam tried to push in like an inquisitive child but Andrea shut it out and pressed a light switch. At least the electricity was on but, of course, it had probably been needed for the occasional vacuuming, and heating in winter. The place did look surprisingly clean with its flagstone floor and light cream plaster walls free of the dust and cobwebs she'd fully expected. She passed the stairs leading to the second floor and looked into the room on her left. Adequately furnished. Enough for a honeymoon couple. No. Forget them. Enough for her own short stay. She walked past the couch and armchair, and stood looking into the large fireplace where half-burned coals rested on the grate. One could almost imagine a fire had burned there recently. She crouched and held out her hand. It actually felt warm. Perhaps the caretaker had confused the dates and lit it yesterday, expecting her. But then why was the gate locked?

She left that room and found herself tiptoeing, as though she were invading someone else's home—someone who had just stepped out and might return at any moment. Nonsense. Andrea planted her feet loudly and firmly as she entered the dining room across the hall, and felt better when she found a thick smudge of dust on her finger after running it across the planks of the old refectory table. She admired the six antique chairs and the large sideboard filled with willow pattern china, and wondered if it would be worth shipping them back to an antique store in San Francisco. That grandfather clock in the corner was a beauty, perhaps she'd keep it for herself. It had stopped at some three o'clock. On the day Lesley died? What a thought! Of course not! She'd wind it later and hear what it sounded like; this place deserved a little life. Stupid to have kept it like a time capsule for all these years.

Achoo! Her own sneeze startled her. Raising her head she sniffed. What was that smell? She'd been conscious of it since first opening the front door and now it seemed stronger. So very familiar, what was it… reminiscent of Berkeley street fairs. Give the place a good airing come morning. She replaced the plate she had been inspecting, went back into the hall and paused, looking toward the forbidding dark door which must lead to the kitchen. Later—she decided—she'd explore the bedrooms first.

After the first three stairs Andrea was stopped on the small landing by the etching of a flowing haired young woman who stood in a field with a lamb in her arms and a ewe pressing against her long, wind-blown skirt. Lesley must have hung that there. Yes. Andrea touched the protective glass. She was sure of it. Well, she would take it down and replace it with something modern. And yet she stayed looking at it, knowing it was the kind of picture she would have loved once; just as she had liked the photos of Lesley... once.

A scuffling sound disturbed the sepulchral quiet. Mice. Bound to be in an old place like this. Get traps tomorrow. Andrea continued up, ducking under the low black beam near the top and wondering how many times tall Robert must have cracked his skull on it.

There were four doors off the narrow passage at the top. She could see bathroom fixtures inside the open one at the end so the others must be to bedrooms. The first she looked into faced the front of the house and was large, with a double bed made up with a comforter dotted with roses, and pillowcases embroidered with the initials RJ and LJ. Andrea stared for a moment then turned to the first of two smaller rooms looking out toward the back. Instantly she knew this would be hers. Here the open white muslin curtains showed moor and sky which was so much the dream of her youth that now she looked out into her own past...

"What can you see from the windows, Robert?"

He took her hand and played with her fingers. "From the back... you'd love it, Andy! The greenest of pastures climb up to moorland that blends into a forever of wild sky. And the weather changes constantly so the view's never the same from one moment to the next. You can't imagine the wonderful sense of space and freedom. An ancient, sure-of-itself kind of distance, different to anything we have here. Oh, Andy, I wish you could see it." He threw his head back with that dreamy, far-away look in his eyes and she trembled with adoration.

"Just keep telling me Robert. I love to hear..."

That's right... he'd called her Andy. When had he stopped? Andrea smoothed the curtain, then gave the hem a small tug. She'd wanted to come here so badly all those years ago and now what was the use? The young romantic was long gone. All that was left was a middle-aged, American widow whose greatest desire was to have her fundraiser well attended. God, what a dismal picture! A gentle melancholy left Andrea staring into space, then she shook her head. Back to business. Must bring in belongings and the groceries.

After laying her handbag and raincoat on the bed she clattered downstairs and out to her car.

It was enough to bring in only one suitcase and the provisions; Robert could stay where he was. She slammed the trunk lid. "Christ!" Her head snapped back as a cloud of rooks whirled and cawed from a nearby elm.

When her heart had stopped racing Andrea glanced around to make sure no one had seen and then laughed at herself. No one here for sure. In fact the rest of the world might as well have fallen off into space. 'Come to think of it there isn't one person who knows exactly where I am—nor cares.' Andrea shrugged, rather liking the idea. 'Mustn't let this place get to me though. Come on, get moving!' And yet she still stood, case in one hand, string bag of groceries in the other, listening, but hearing nothing—no sound of vehicles on the road, no distant voice, not even a dog's bark.

Sudden wind spattered water from an overhanging branch onto the roof of her car, tapping like impatient fingers.

Andrea clucked her tongue and marched briskly back into the house. Scarcely pausing she set her case down at the foot of the stairs and continued on toward the kitchen. The dark door swung heavily inward from her push and her footsteps echoed on the flagstone floor as she crossed to the table in the center of the room. Only then did she stop to look around her at the five high backed chairs, ancient gas stove, small sink and, against one wall, a surprisingly used-looking, lumpy sofa. Some strange configuration under the table made her look more closely and she was amused to find that the top could be lifted to offer a bathtub.

There were two other doors, one probably led to a pantry. Through a window in the other she could see the garden. And there in the kitchen's darkest corner was a small refrigerator. Thank heaven for that! She kept her mind busy, warding off an uneasiness that kept trying to interrupt her matter-of-fact progress. She pressed a finger against her top lip, forestalling another sneeze, and wondered if it was her imagination or if that strange smell really was growing stronger.

Taking butter and milk from the bag she opened the fridge door, but relief from seeing the light go on, quickly switched to surprise as she saw the bowl of eggs and jug of milk already resting on the rack. Perhaps the caretaker had put them there for her. But when she opened the vegetable drawer and found half a wilted lettuce, three limp carrots and several sprouting potatoes, all those weird feelings she had so far kept at bay zoomed in on her. Tentatively one hand reached out to touch the withered vegetables as though she hoped to find they were really a mirage.

"Wot the 'ell d'you think you're doin'?"

Her hand sprang back and her heart almost leaped out of her body for the second time in the past half hour. Her thoughts whirled. Then commonsense took over. The elusive Simpson had finally arrived. Deliberately she finished placing her belongings on the rack, then slowly turned, ready to give him the lambasting he deserved for startling her, using her fridge, and leaving the gate locked so she'd gotten soaked and… the words died on her lips as she stared into glaring eyes drawn into devilish shape with thick black eyeliner, lids a startling green. Above them glowering black eyebrows almost joined in the middle of a single perpendicular frown line and the head was shaved bare but for a row of brown hair that stood stiffly upright from front to back. From one of this creature's ears hung an oversize safety pin and from his smirking, orange-painted mouth dangled one of the marijuana cigarettes Andrea had been smelling since her arrival.

CHAPTER ELEVEN

They called them punks back home. You gave them wide berth when you passed them on Main Street swaggering up the sidewalk or hanging out at the local coffee house or ice cream store, discordant music blasting from somewhere close by. Andrea always looked on them with disgust and wondered what their parents were thinking. Now, after the surprise wore off, this one, in the uniform of ill-fitting, mismatched clothes and heavy boots, stirred the same reaction.

"What are you doing, would be more to the point," she snapped. "I'm Mrs. James and this is my house. If you're the caretaker's son I think you'd better tell your parents to come on over. I'd like to talk to them."

"I'm no one's son. I live 'ere." No more than five-eight the young man stood solid as a rock, emanating animosity like some demonic gargoyle.

Andrea squelched a nervous sinking in her stomach and lifted her chin a notch higher. "Then you're trespassing. We'll see what the police have to say."

"Nay, we'll not."

His solid defiance was unnerving and Andrea wished she'd had more experience with this kind of person so she'd know how to handle the situation. He was only a boy; look at those pimples under his chalky makeup. "Just you wait and see, young man, you'd better not try to bully me." She marched past him down the hall, desperately trying to remember if she'd seen a phone out there. But before she could get far he dodged ahead and leaned again the wall blocking her way with an expression so insolent her hand itched to slap him. He took a drag at his cigarette and blew sweet smelling smoke in her face.

She controlled her fury. Even boys could be dangerous. "You're stupid to smoke that stuff. It'll fry your brains. Now get out of my way."

But he didn't. They stared at each other. A sound came from the other room like a coal falling in the grate. He really has been living here she thought. What am I going to do? I don't know the laws or who to speak to, or how violent someone like this can get. He can't just let me walk out... what can I do?

But the boy had already decided and she watched as he leaned down to his right boot and slowly withdrew a slim, long bladed knife which he wiped deliberately across his palm.

Andrea allowed herself one discrete step backward and tasted fear. But he's only a kid, she told herself for the umpteenth time. "You're heading for a pack of trouble," she said. "The police won't treat pulling a knife lightly, y'know." Annoyingly her voice came out higher than usual, but then the boy was surely as scared as she was.

He grinned, showing two sharp incisors, and Andrea quickly scrubbed that last supposition. "Wot makes you think they'll know? Place were left deserted. I got squatters rights, I 'ave." His voice broke a couple of times and his dark eyes glared and sparked from their massacred surroundings. "T'house be mine."

Run. Just get out of here. Thoughts jumped like startled grasshoppers in Andrea's head. He may be young but he could also be crazy and that knife was a man's. Humor him. Find someone... find the caretaker...

The knife pointed toward her stomach which suddenly became flatter than it had been in years. "Don't go expecting no caretaker, neither. He died years ago."

As though he'd read her mind. She didn't like that...

"I been collecting the checks down at the post office. I got yer cable too. No one ever comes by this place lest I ask 'em. They knows better, so don't expect nowt in the way of help."

Andrea's heart sank and she fought to keep her usual

confidence. "That's your food in the fridge?" she asked more to hear her own voice than anything.

"Aye. So's wot you just put in. Everything's mine in this house."

She couldn't take her eyes off that steel blade. There were such stories in the papers these days. Careful. Don't upset him. Did marijuana excite or calm...? The silence grew unbearable. "Well, what are you going to do? We can't stand here all day."

The knife wavered, and for a moment she thought she saw indecision in the tremble of his lip, but he made a beckoning motion. "Upstairs." It was the same rehearsed snarl he'd used since the beginning. A familiar sound. Bogart... Or Bronson... "Upstairs," he repeated.

"Upstairs?" Surely this skinny little punk wouldn't try to rape her!

But he grabbed her arm with a strength that hurt and pushed her in the right direction, following with the knife pressed to her waist.

Her suitcase sat in the way like an innocent bystander and somehow, just seeing it revived Andrea's courage. "Why not let me take this and go? I'll promise not to say anything. I hadn't planned to stay long anyway..."

"And we'd never 'ear from you again? Could just go on living 'ere as if you'd never come?"

"Sure, why not?" said Andrea eagerly, sliding her fingers through the handle. "I'll just quietly go home."

The jab in her ribs made her gasp.

"Girt, gaumless bitch! You think I'm a fool? I don't trust no one, I don't. Upstairs and stop acting so bloody pompous. Your kind allus thinks everyone's stupid—it's you that's daft as a brush! Move!"

Frightened by his anger Andrea stumbled to the stairs, suitcase banging against her leg. This couldn't really be happening! She climbed as quickly as she could, feeling the prick of his knife every time she faltered. Would she find a hole in her jacket later... damn, she'd had trouble finding this shade too. Automatically she went into the room she had chosen previously. The door slammed behind her and when she turned she was alone.

"You'll not try to leave if tha knows wot's good for thee," came the snarl from the other side.

Andrea stood still. Silence. Stealthily she tiptoed back and lifted the latch. The door opened two inches, five. Wham! A steel blade quivered in the wood next to her head.

She gasped, then couldn't breathe as her heart repeated the thud of the blade. Shocked by her weakness she leaned with her back against the solid wood and tried to reassemble her thoughts as she pulled a tissue from her sleeve and wiped her forehead. The always cool, calm Mrs. James had allowed herself to be intimidated by a mere, pot smoking child! It was ridiculous! A joke! No one back home must ever hear of it! But now she had to get out of this asinine situation. Surely someone would drop by. If only she'd stopped at the post office when she'd driven in as she'd planned. Even the car rental place only had her home address and wouldn't worry how long she kept their wretched vehicle—would just keep happily charging it to her credit card. Damn! Damn! She hadn't managed things well at all. But of course… the car… sooner or later someone would see it parked out front and come to inquire! Oh let it be sooner! She'd never needed anyone else's help before, but of course there'd always been Robert although she'd never thought of it at the time.

She walked into the middle of the room, wet and cold and stiff. 'God, is that me?' Her eye had been caught by her misshapen image in the wavy glass that hung over the chipped black chest of drawers. 'What a mess!' Like a magnet the mirror drew her, and as she tried to push her bedraggled hair into shape she looked for the place that distorted her least. The woman who looked back was a pale, disheveled stranger, the kind who would be in a situation like this…

The roar of an engine distracted her.

A car! Rescue!

She dashed to the window, reaching it just in time to see her own Escort backing rapidly around the side of the house. It stopped beside a shed off to the right, and the punk got out. It was very quiet now and with a sinking heart Andrea watched him swagger off, tossing and catching her keys. How stupid of her to have left them on that hall table. Her eyes stung with frustration. There must be something she could do, some way to escape. If she thought hard enough she'd find it then first thing in the morning she'd go to a hairdresser.

CHAPTER TWELVE

Andrea opened the window, and leaned out, looking down into a garden tousled with violets and primroses, marigolds, snowdrops and yellow and blue crocus, all sprinkled amidst shaggy, untended grass. Near the house was a plot scarcely less wild but instead of flowers the heads of cabbages, radish and chard showed between the weeds. And against the wall beneath her, hollyhocks nodded under rain that had again begun to fall with the murmur of a distant crowd. Andrea breathed deeply. Sweet, how very sweet it smelled…

"What kind of a garden did Lesley plan to have?"

She and Robert relaxed under a tree on campus. His head rested in her lap and she twisted a strand of his dark hair between her fingers.

He squinted up into the branches. "I think she'd leave it quite wild, with masses of flowers everywhere and fruit trees for us and the birds to share. What d'you think?"

"Oh, yes. She'd like forget-me-nots and violets and lily of the valley— and roses. Lots of roses."

"Unpruned."

"Of course. And a vegetable garden…"

Robert pulled Andrea's face down to his and kissed her…

Sunshine wove through this latest shower turning it light and shimmering. A rainbow arched, one end fading into the elms at the bottom of the garden as a breeze carried the scent of fresh, wet soil, honeysuckle and something special swept in from the moor. A bee buzzed from flower to flower, then up to the rose that almost reached Andrea's window. For a moment he hovered by the crimson bud, then darted away. Andrea had the oddest feeling. The one she'd gotten when, as a child, she'd opened a new book of fairy tales—that magical invitation to a new world.

Dark clouds rolled northward to lie along the top of the distant skyline, and the rainbow disappeared. A cold wind whipped the curtains. Andrea remembered her reason for looking out in the first place and carefully searched, but it was much too far to jump, and there was no possible way to climb. She pulled back into the room and closed the casement, tensing at the sound it made, and listening for any reaction from downstairs. Nothing. She sat on the edge of the bed to think but couldn't come up with one good idea.

Evening approached and as shadows took over the corners Andrea had to admit that for once she had no control.

There was nothing to do but wait. Surely the punk must leave sooner or later and then she would escape to that cottage on the other side of the bridge and borrow their phone. She shivered. Might as well get into dry clothes.

Stealthily she brought the one chair and jammed its back under the door latch for security, then she exchanged her rain soaked suit and shoes for a skirt, woolen sweater and slippers. After her discarded clothes were neatly hung over the metal rail at the end of the bed to dry, she combed her hair and put on lipstick. Then she bustled about the room, drawing the curtains, stuffing kleenex into her wet shoes, and laying one of her designer scarves over the candlewick bedspread to protect her head from germs. She placed her suitcase in the corner, handbag on top, then changed her mind and decided to keep the handbag with her. Finally she went to the door and pressed her ear against it. She heard distant music, otherwise all was quiet. She tested the handle and the chair held firm.

She'd nap for a while, then she'd demand dinner. That decision made, she carefully lay on top of the bed, slippers neatly placed on the floor, a cardigan pulled over her feet and knees, handbag alongside.

Very soon the only sound in the room was gentle breathing, while downstairs the kitchen throbbed to a cacophony of hard rock.

When she awoke Andrea quickly reacquainted herself with her situation. The room, peppery with darkness, seemed utterly peaceful and she began to believe she had over-reacted to the boy's threats. She'd probably suffered a little from jetlag, despite her precautions, and it had led to an overactive imagination and lack of her usual level headedness. She would leave now. She turned on the light. Unfortunately the punk had her car keys but she would get someone to take her to the nearest Inn and call the police from there, then come back with them. She'd charge him with car theft also. While she planned her moves she fumbled through her case for some comfortable, soft soled shoes. Every now and then, as she put them on, she paused to listen. Nothing. The house was either empty or its intruder asleep, possibly on that sofa in the kitchen. She carefully combed her still damp hair and powdered her nose. Moved the barrier from the door. About to leave she put her hand on her suitcase but no, she'd be back. Oh how good it would be to see that awful hoodlum hauled away! She'd press all the charges she could and get him locked up for as long as possible. He'd not terrorize anyone else for a very long time.

She opened the door a crack and listened. Nothing. He and his buddies were probably laughing somewhere right now about how he'd scared a silly Yank. Bastard! She should have grabbed that knife away from him, called his bluff. He'd never have had the guts to really hurt her.

Andrea tiptoed into the passageway. Trying to ignore the unfamiliar shadows and creaks of the ancient floorboards she reached the stairs with growing confidence—felt for the first, the second, then the third.

"Newt! Newt!" Shouts ricocheted.

Andrea stumbled. Only her grasp on the banister stopped her from falling into the dark shape that bolted from where it had lurked on the landing. It crashed to the bottom shouting, "She's away! She's away!"

Lights flashed on. Andrea blinked, blinded and only just able to make out the grotesque, painted face looking up at her. A bearded old man hovered behind the boy. "Where do you think you're off to, woman? Tell me. Where? Speak will ye!"

All Andrea could see through her astonishment was the punk's crimson mouth opening, closing, distorting.

"Didn't you 'ear me say you was to stay put? Are ye deaf as well as daft? You do what I say in this house, woman! You 'ear me?"

The punk's strident harangue scraped every nerve, and Andrea found herself screaming back at him. "Stupid? You call me stupid? You're the one who's going to jail. You can't go around living in other people's houses and imprisoning them. Don't you think someone's going to come looking for me? I'm not a nobody you know!" She glared into those wildly made up eyes and couldn't care less what happened. Boldly she began to descend.

The old man clutched and pulled at the punk's jacket and the boy half turned to him, eyes still on Andrea. "Go to the kitchen, Pops, get yoursel' a cup a tea. It'll be alright."

The old man gave Andrea one last desperate look and fled.

She came down, step after step; confident, superior, and furious.

"Get the 'ell back in yer room." The boy half crouched, voice a snarl. "Go on, get yersel' fuckin' back up there!"

He had his knife out but she knew he wouldn't use it. She reached the bottom, hand outstretched to shove him aside if need be, then something stopped her; something gold on the floor a few paces behind him. Robert's box.

The punk glanced around to see what she stared at; looked at her face suddenly pale and irresolute, then jumped backward, snatched up the glinting container and flaunted it in front of her. Encouraged by her obvious distress he leered and did a wild dance around the passageway, swooping the box over and around and up and down. "Wot's the matter, Lady. Summat important is it?" He finally stopped, panting.

"You had no right to take that…"

"So wotcha goin' to do about it? Mebbe I'd better 'ave a look, eh?"

"Leave it alone. Please."

"Why should I?"

"It's my husband."

"Wot guff is that?"

"It's true. It's his ashes."

"Well, I'll be fair capped!" David shook the box, then looked slyly at Andrea. "Yer 'usband's really in 'ere?" He held his knife to the paper.

"I said so didn't I? Give it to me!" She ran the last two steps then stopped short as the blade hovered ready to plunge.

"Stop!" she screamed.

"Cutting into this'd upset you something dreadful, wouldn't it. Mebbe we can come to an agreement 'ere."

"Agreement?"

"You just go back upstairs and be a good missus and hubby'll stay safe. Any trouble and pfft, 'e's out."

Andrea stared, speechless, but she knew Robert would win. He always did.

"Well, missus, 'ow's that for a reason to be'ave? Better get on up now, I'm short on patience."

Andrea hesitated for only a fraction of an instant, then she turned and trudged back upstairs. "I'll win in the end," she muttered, fighting the tremor in her voice.

"It's now I cares about."

From the top she took a last look down at the odd looking creature with the gold box under his arm. "Keep him safe." All her confidence and anger had crumbled and this last effort at authority wheezed like the final gasp of air from a balloon.

"Long as you try nothin'. Oh, by the way, you c'n use the

bathroom. Can't 'ave you messing on the floor, can we?"

The taunting, triumphant laugh that followed made Andrea close her eyes and stiffen with rage. How she hated this vile boy for his disrespect, and for his assurance that she'd do anything to save her husband's ashes. She hated him even more because he was right. Why couldn't she break that pact? Why did it hold her like a cement block? She looked past her captor to the door leading to freedom. Everyone would say it wasn't worth staying here for a pile of dust. And Robert would agree with them. They'd call her a fool—but they didn't understand—when a promise was burned into you so deeply; when it was all that had kept you going for so long... no one could understand. That last part of Robert held her as firmly as a pair of handcuffs. If she failed there it would make everything else worthless. Shoulders sagging she retreated to the simple bathroom that had only a toilet and a cold water sink.

No sooner had she closed the door than she threw up, violently and painfully, and as she retched she prayed that the punk couldn't hear her. Finally, weak, sweating and shivering, she dashed icy water onto her face, again and again, as though it could wash away all that had happened, then she sank onto the closed toilet seat, her head in her hands.

Eventually she sighed and pushed her hair back from her forehead. Things would work out. Of course they would. Meantime she must make herself comfortable. The light was out in the hall now but she found the switches in the other two bedrooms and collected anything she might need; moth-eaten but useable blankets, sheets that still smelled faintly of lavender, a couple of pillow cases she could use as towels. She didn't even try to be quiet. "To hell with him," she thought as she carried her booty back to her room and directed a last glare toward the empty staircase. "Tomorrow's another day, young man," she thought as she slammed her door as loudly as she could.

The next ten minutes were spent making her bed. She turned the feather mattress, smoothed a double layer of sheets over it, then put on the upper one, with hospital corners, and three blankets, a fourth folded at the foot of the final coverlet. She fluffed the pillow, feeling as though each step toward her own comfort was a blow at her captor, and when she had finished she stepped back and viewed her work with satisfaction.

A sound interrupted and drew her to the window. There in the garden, bathed in light from the open kitchen door, someone bent, picking chard. A golden braid fell to one side, almost reaching the ground, and Andrea immediately noticed the crisp yellow ribbon at its end, oddly incongruous to the ragged, baggy grey sweater and worn blue jeans that comprised the rest of the outfit. The figure straightened, looking toward the dark moor like a startled fawn, then it abruptly turned and ran inside. As the light hit her face Andrea recognized the girl she'd seen that morning on the bridge. It seemed like days ago.

CHAPTER THIRTEEN

That evening became one of the longest in Andrea's life. Left with nothing to do, nagging hunger allowed visions of food to fill her mind. She tried to busy herself by going over everything that had happened and imagining better ways she could have handled it—but the final decision was that there wasn't much else she could have done—and her thoughts returned to eating.

"Thoughtless pigs!" She yanked back the curtain and looked down from her window at the light that bled from the kitchen. They were probably having dinner now—that unlikely trio—a young woman, an old man and a teenager from a horror movie. Who on earth were they? Surely at least one of them must have a grain of humanity and would bring her something... just a piece of chicken. Steak would be better. Even a sandwich! She strained for the sound of approaching footsteps, the rattle of dishes on a tray... well, to hell with them all, she'd go to bed.

Fully clothed Andrea stretched out under the top blanket. "I should have eaten more in that tea room—what did I have anyway? Soup. I should have had a sandwich, at least." She flung back the blanket and wandered around the dark room, then sat on the chair and stared at the silhouette of a tree.

Time passed. Sounds from outside were unfamiliar and in the cottage it was dead quiet. Was everyone in bed? She thought about sneaking downstairs and getting something to eat—but no, there'd been that couch in the corner where she suspected the boy might sleep. What was that? Music? She opened the door a crack and was assaulted by a blast of sound—raucous, horrible stuff that would have shaken her house in California, but this place was too solid... she shut the noise out but the beat remained—persistent—nagging. "How can they enjoy themselves while I'm starving to death!" She'd never been this hungry—except once—at boarding school when she'd been reduced to eating toothpaste while confined to her room without dinner. She couldn't recall why she was being punished but she did remember deciding that if she ever had children she'd discipline them with a good spanking and get it over with, never starvation and boredom. She must have subconsciously followed her childhood plan because she never had disciplined her son by sending him to his room. Of course she'd been so busy there'd been nursery school and baby sitters... what had they done? No, she would have known had Leslie ever been punished that way... surely...

For a moment she had forgotten her cramping stomach. Well, she wouldn't eat toothpaste but maybe there was something... she grabbed her purse and rummaged through it, coming out triumphantly with a package of Lifesavers. As she sat on the bed crunching them she thought of all the women who purposely went without dinner to lose weight and decided one night certainly wouldn't hurt her, but an unbidden thought whispered, "What if they don't feed me tomorrow? Or the next day?"

To defy the chill that shuddered down her spine, she turned on the light. "If I'd done that sooner they might have noticed it and remembered me," she chided herself. But now she was too late, there was no more music. They were probably asleep. She glanced at her watch. Six? Impossible! She put it to her ear. Shook it. Nothing. A black wave of true panic swept over Andrea. That loss of measured time that kept her days in order struck her as the ultimate desertion, an abandonment that left her floating in a void. "Please," she murmured as she wound and shook the pretty piece of gold and glass, "Please!" But the wretched thing denied her one second more. Perhaps it had drowned in the rain as she'd battled to open the gate, perhaps it would dry out tomorrow... but deep inside Andrea knew it wouldn't; time as she knew it was forever finished and she must step alone into an unmeasured future.

"Hell, hell, hell." She snapped off the light and lay back on the bed, her eyes open, staring at nothing. Such silence. Once she thought she heard a car and sat up, but no lights gave away the position of it or any other signs of human life. An owl hooted softly and she could see stars through her window. One moved blinking across the sky and she imagined the people sitting in that airplane completely unaware of her predicament. She'd probably be up there in a few days looking back on this as an experience to tell Leslie. When they released her tomorrow she'd scatter Robert's ashes and get away as quickly as possible. Some realtor could clean up the property and sell it. Everything would return to normal in the morning...

Three raps startled her into daylight. Thank goodness I slept in my clothes, was her first thought as she scrambled out of bed, but when she got to the door she hesitated. A few moments passed and when the knock was not repeated she cautiously lifted the latch and peered out. On the floor was a tray with a cup of tea and some gluey oatmeal. Eagerly, and overwhelmed with relief, she picked it up, carried it into her room and sat on the edge of the bed. They were going to feed her! Each spoonful of porridge was delicious and the warmth of the tea comforting. Sunshine filtered through the curtains and outside birds sang.

Andrea put the tray on the dresser and remade the bed. Next she went down the hall and had a sponge bath, shrinking from the cold water but feeling better afterward. Back in her room, with the help of her own small mirror, she applied several layers of makeup, carefully did her eyes, her lips and her cheeks, then combed, styled and sprayed her hair. She put on her black suit, accessorized it with a dusty-rose scarf at her neck, small diamond earrings, black stockings, and high heels. During all this time she had not allowed her thoughts to touch on yesterday's embarrassing defeat, nor did she think of the punk except as a youth she would shortly deal with. She looked in the big mirror and, ignoring the glass's idiosyncrasies, saw Mrs. Andrea James. "Time to go," she said, and opening the door marched to the top of the stairs.

"Young man?" she called.

The painted face sneered up at her almost immediately but this time she was ready, and although she held firmly to the banister her feet met each step firmly and confidently. I am Andrea James, American, Chairman of the Cancer Fund, Director of the Arts Council, first woman president of our Rotary club.

"Come to inquire about Mr. James, 'ave you?" the punk interrupted her thoughts, leaning nonchalantly against the wall stroking the calico cat in his arms. "Slept very well, thank you, not a peep out of 'im."

Andrea stared haughtily into his grin. "Have you no respect for the dead? Didn't your mother teach you anything?"

"Dead or alive I treat folk as I see 'em. I never knew your mister so why should I respect 'im? Just 'cause 'e died's no reason; we can all die." He shrugged, let the cat drop to the floor, and took out a cigarette. Casually he lit it, then blew smoke so it rose in a blue haze up the stairwell. "I mean your old man might 'ave been a right bugger for all I know."

Andrea longed to strike him, she was close enough now, but instead it was he who pounced, darting a lightening blow to the side of her face, then back across the other cheek with his knuckles so that she fell against the railing. She clung there, stunned, every thought knocked from her head. His face loomed and she stared into his inhuman eyes as though hypnotized.

"Listen close now." His voice was low thunder, throbbing with menace. "I will toss them ashes. Believe me, it's up to you. Don't you ever come down them stairs again."

She searched that face for someone to reason with, but could see only paint.

The lips moved again, "Quick as a flash 'e'll be gone if you don't stay put. An' then I'll be after you and you won't look like much when they find you, if they ever do. Get upstairs. Get!" His voice had risen to a bellow, mixing with the pain and taste of blood in Andrea's mouth. Thoughtless she scrambled back to her room, slammed the door and slumped against it gasping. He'd hit her! No one had ever hit her! He could kill her too, she believed it now—and he'd certainly have no compunction about throwing Robert out. "Oh God, it hurts!" She touched her swollen lip and approached the mirror, then recoiled from what she saw. With her smudged mascara and lipstick, swelling, and beginning bruises, she looked as grotesque as he did! Half sobbing she snatched cleanser and tissue from her make-up bag and painfully cleansed her face of every trace of make up. She dabbed peroxide on her lip, grateful to its sting for fending off panic, then she sat on the bed, hands around her knees, rocking.

Distant voices rose in anger. She swayed forward and stayed there. Then the punk's voice came closer, making her break out in a cold sweat. "You let 'er pass and it's yer necks," she heard from the foot of the stairs. "You 'ear me, both of you? She makes one wrong move and you dump that there gold box and kill 'er if y' have to. She'd be a sight less trouble under a few foot of soil in the garden, for certain, but we'll give 'er a chance. It's up to both of you to watch, mind, day and night."

There followed a mumble of assent.

He'd spoken on purpose for her to hear, that Andrea knew, but learning that the others were behind him left her drained of strength and filled with despair. Once she walked around the room only to slump back onto the bed, to stare unseeingly at the floor. "What on earth am I to do?" she whispered.

Somehow she slept, fitfully, but long enough to awake with a modicum of renewed optimism. Stiff and sore as her face was, after careful inspection during which her mood vacillated between fear and outrage, she decided no permanent damage had been done. She should bathe it though, get the swelling down. Wasn't there a vase in the front bedroom that would hold cold water, and something to rip into rags? Confidently she crossed the hall but the door was locked. Impossible! She tried the other room, but that door also refused to budge. She rattled the handles in disbelief. Someone had been upstairs! It was not so much the fact that the rooms were closed off that undid her, but that someone had invaded what she considered her safe haven.

Back in her own room she tilted the chair against the door, and for the first time really felt like a prisoner. At least she had her own things with her and maybe starting a letter to Leslie would make her feel less alone. She found her writing pad, and after retrieving a pen from her purse began: Dear Leslie... you'll never believe this... she stopped. How ludicrous! So melodramatic and unlike her! He'd think she'd gone mad! Andrea threw the pen down and went to the window. Lifting it open she sat on the sill and watched bees fumble in and out of the hollyhocks. The sun was warm and she closed her eyes listening to sounds familiar from peaceful days. Buzzing, trilling, mooing and bleating. She and Robert had spent one of their first weekends up at Bodega Bay on the California coast, and had walked through early morning foggy fields.

"I imagine the moors are like this, aren't they?"

He'd looked down at her and grinned, rather sadly she'd thought. "Yes, my little Andy, they are—quite similar. Come on, let's run!"

And they had, her hair bouncing on her shoulders and curling, fringed with mist around her face. They'd come to a gate where two dewy faced kittens sat in the grass mewing up at them. They'd each picked one up to pet and she'd noticed the tender expression that came over Robert's face and assumed he was thinking of Lesley. She'd quickly set her kitten down and suggested they go back for breakfast.

Andrea left the window and walked around the room. She straightened things, tried to nap, but the hours dragged unbearably and she travelled through stages of anger, frustration, loneliness and, when her lip or bruises reminded her, fear. She brooded about the punk, stirring up hatred for him and a desire for revenge. Sometimes she thought she could hear him coming for her and then she grew cold with terror until she could prove to herself he was nowhere near. In the afternoon she was horrified to discover she had bitten off two fingernails. 'Thinking will drive me crazy! Must find something to do—a book—in my suitcase...'

Searching through her belongings she came across the picture of Lesley Clayton. A familiar face—thank God! She put it on the dresser. Even the steady gaze of her rival was welcome company now.

When the sun began to drop behind the rim of the moor the old man brought her a tray. She recognized his approaching footsteps and opened the door to accept the soup made with vegetables, probably from the garden, and a piece of the bread she'd bought yesterday. He seemed nervous, keeping his head with its mass of wild white hair bowed, only darting quick looks at her with surprisingly blue eyes.

"When will that crazy punk let me go?" she asked. "What's he going to do?" She spat the word "punk" like an oath, telling herself she would never think of him as a boy again.

But the old man gave no intimation he'd heard her—just turned and went back down the stairs leaving Andrea to wonder if he were deaf or just plain stubborn. No not deaf, she thought when she heard his voice answering the girl's as he entered the kitchen. The kitchen where Robert's ashes held her hostage. I should call that monster's bluff and leave Robert, I know I should. I could escape alone if I really tried. I don't know a woman who wouldn't call me a fool not to.

She kicked the door shut and plunked the tray on the dresser so she sat facing the girl in the picture. "But you understand. You know I'd never rest if anything happened to him now. After all these years I've got to bring our deal to its conclusion. I've just got to!" She dipped into the soup and ate her meal under Lesley's steady gaze as she had done so many times in the past.

"What a surprise!" Robert had exclaimed on that first

birthday after their marriage. She'd racked her brains for the finest present she could think of, and as sacrifice made it even greater, she had taken the best negatives of Lesley she could find, had them printed and the prints framed then wrapped in a big box tied with blue ribbon and put by Robert's place at the breakfast table. She had sat there trying to ignore the jealousy that churned in her breast as she watched him look at each photo, but it was worth it when he took her in his arms and carried her back up to the big bed. "Oh, my silly little Andrea," he had breathed into her hair.

He was very late for work that day and after he left she had gone through the house placing the pictures where she thought he would like them.

Funny, she'd forgotten all that… she lowered the spoon back into the now empty soup bowl and remembered how wonderful it had been to be young and in love.

CHAPTER FOURTEEN

The next two days were identical, alone but for Lesley's photographic presence and the old man's morning and evening visits. From what she could guess he came at about nine and five, and the time between seemed interminable. She began to look forward to his arrival, the only thing that gave her day meaning and anchored it to reality, and each time she tried to cajole him into talking. "What's your name?" "Will it get warmer soon?" "Why does he keep me here?" But to her frustration she could summon no reaction from behind that white beard.

She tried everything then finally she lost her temper. "Dammit, are you an idiot or something? You could at least be civil! Letting a dumb kid order you about!"

Perhaps it was imagination that made her think the gnarled hands hesitated before handing over the tray but still he uttered no sound, and she slammed the door after him. "Why don't you fall and break your bloody neck!" she shouted, hating him as he descended the stairs and left her alone again.

Then she spent the rest of the day worrying that he might have heard and refuse to bring her another meal.

He did come but now her silence matched his.

Hunger nagged almost constantly but at least emotional exhaustion allowed her to take frequent naps to pass the time. At first, she spent hours planning escapes and ways to rescue Robert's ashes. She wrote useless ideas in her notebook and even detailed the times and means of her return to San Francisco and home. Every so often she would tiptoe to the top of the stairs thinking this was the time she would find no one home and could retrieve Robert and get away but always, as though by magic, someone appeared at the bottom. If it were the old man she'd glare at him and stamp angrily back to her room. If it were the punk she'd rush back to slam the door against the torrent of obscenities that would crash up the stairs and along the hall after her. How she despised him! He didn't seem human. But it wasn't until the fourth night, when she'd heard no one for hours yet was still thwarted by the girl's baleful glare and her squeal to alert the others, that she gave up. She couldn't beat the three of them.

Defeated, she leaned against her door, head bowed, whimpering small childlike sounds that frightened her because they were so alien. Guitar music seeped through her dark thoughts. She raised her head to listen, then drifted to the window and pushed the curtain aside so as to lean her cheek against the cold glass. The sky was huge and filled with stars. She could do nothing for Robert or herself—after all her years of strength she was a failure. But what difference did it make— really? The music continued, soft, soothing. What reason was there for her to do anything? The thought uncurled like a sprout from winter's soil. Who cared? Andrea drew in a deep breath, then let it out to fog her own reflection. It was as though a wearisome weight lifted from her soul.

For the first time she undressed, put on her nightgown and got completely into bed, where she sank into a deep sleep lulled by the music that played on and on.

Dawn brought a hubbub of distant sounds she hadn't noticed before: A rooster crowed, cows bawled, a dog yipped and the garden harbored a symphony of birdsong. As a breeze rattled the window Andrea snuggled deeper into the feather mattress, pulling bedclothes over her head, curled safely in her own warm darkness. Nowhere to go, nothing to do, no one to please. What bliss! Early in their marriage she'd trained herself never to sleep in, even on holidays, lest Robert think she waited for him to make love to her. After all he had done exceptionally well at pretending to enjoy her in the beginning. Now she could doze as long as she wanted.

When she finally did get up she ate the waiting breakfast in her robe, then slowly dressed. She was like a convalescent after a long illness, well but still restricted to a life without decisions or duties. She didn't even feel hungry anymore—her stomach must have accustomed itself to the two meals—and above all she was saved from the dreaded moment of finally relinquishing the last of Robert to "her". Andrea smiled at the luxury of it all and as she pottered about the room making her bed and putting away clothes, her thoughts dreamed and drifted, sometimes on things past, sometimes into the unknown world outside.

She was standing by the window when the young woman appeared and began to pull weeds. Andrea moved to one side so as to watch but remain unseen. Such a strange, delicate creature, so thin, with eyes, when she looked up into the trees as she often did, much too big for that small face haloed by golden hair braided into control down her back. Today a red ribbon was neatly tied to its end. A brave splash of color. Andrea watched the grubby hands pull and fling, feeling the dirt on her own hands, up one row and down the next. Every now and then a snatch of song escaped. Andrea almost deciphered the tune several times but it always slipped away and returned as a hint of something else.

Suddenly all motion stopped as the girl tilted her head to listen. Andrea strained to hear what she heard but could make out nothing in particular. Still the girl stood, head cocked, attentive. Such an elfin creature and yet... Andrea peered at the bulky masculine clothes, and then suddenly she knew... the child, for that's what she really was, was pregnant! It was the sometimes awkward movement, and the way she stretched with one hand to her back that gave her away. And now as she stood in the sun, palm resting on the beginning mound below her breasts, a smile formed as though she felt the baby kick—and Andrea also smiled.

Without warning the girl ran into the house—feet skimming the path as though there were no ground.

The garden was barren without her. Even the birds seemed to hush. Who had fathered the baby? The punk? Good Lord no—such a coupling was unthinkable, besides she was much older than he. She appeared so innocent. Perhaps some stranger, wild and free as she was had passed through the village. A brief passionate love affair... then thrown out by her parents.

Andrea, satisfied by this explanation, turned her thoughts to the hills and tried to imagine what it would be like to walk up there where the colors were more gold than green. Closer, in the low meadows, sheep grazed with smaller white specks beside them, and the high pitched bleat of lambs and the deeper call of their mothers came soft or louder according to the direction of the wind. What would it be like to pet a lamb? Would one let her? "Did they let you?" she asked Lesley's picture. "I expect you knew all these fields. What a wonderful place to grow up in." Lesley gazed past her through the window.

For two days Andrea enjoyed her peace. Watching the girl was enough entertainment and she grew attached to her, thinking of her more as something out of a fairy tale or a dream than human flesh and blood. She'd smile as the strange little creature ran up and down the overgrown paths, sometimes laughing aloud, sometimes stopping to crouch and carry on earnest conversation with some blossom, reaching out to stroke a bud or collect a drop of dew and put it to her lips. Often she would hum that strange almost recognizable tune. It was like watching a being made of mist, something that might vanish in an instant. And then one afternoon Andrea remembered how when she'd been five or six years old she'd had an imaginary playmate very like this. Could this be that childhood companion returned to her. "What nonsense," Andrea thought, but then shrugged, "Why not? I can think whatever I like. I'll probably wake up any minute and find the whole thing's a dream anyway."

When the garden was empty Andrea would often lie on her bed following the movement of clouds across the sky, thoughts idly wandering, and her day began and ended with the quiet footsteps of the old man.

CHAPTER FIFTEEN

Then all at once on the seventh day it wasn't enough just to look at the fields anymore. She wanted to be there, touch a lamb, hear the wind through the grass, feel the rough stones in the walls. She was all slept out and could spend no more time napping. She began to fret. Was she fated never to set foot on this land she'd spent her girlhood dreaming about? This land that had vicariously molded her life? That night she tossed, weary of her prison, and bored.

Morning sun stroked its way along the tops then slid down sleek flanks of hillside to brighten the gullies and glisten on fresh young leaves of beech, sycamore and larch. Caught up in beauty Andrea felt a twinge of annoyance at being interrupted by the footsteps bringing breakfast.

Knuckles rapped on door.

She flung it open. Damned old fool! All her frustration focused on the man who stood meekly in front of her. No name. No speech. A nonentity. Her warder. "You are a real pain, you know that? You and your creeping and silence. Wouldn't kill you to be civil, would it? I didn't ask to be kept here, y'know." His passivity left her free to say anything and she wanted to hurt. "I used to dream of being in a place like this. I thought Yorkshire people would be interesting and romantic like in Wuthering Heights. Ha, what a laugh! If you and he," she jabbed a finger floorward, "are any example—a couple of useless, lazy squatters. I bet you never even noticed that fantastic sunrise just now. Oh, hell, give me that!"

She grabbed the tray but was surprised so find it firmly held, then even more startled by the sternness in clear eyes suddenly fixed on hers. "Maybe we're not so bad as you think, Woman. Don't judge what you know nowt about." His eyelids lowered and he released the tray. At the head of the stairs he stopped. "You know, I don't remember Heathcliff being all that sociable." He continued out of sight leaving Andrea staring at his back.

She reentered her room with a feeling of triumph. She had finally gotten him to talk! But the mood soon passed. She was still alone. Waiting… for what? She sighed and gloom filled the pit of her stomach. She pined for something she'd once had and lost. Someone who cared. Dammit there was no one! "All I want are a few words to tell me everything's going to be all right," she whispered to the unresponsive Lesley.

That evening it rained, not the showers of previous nights, but a solid thundering downpour that spilled from the eaves in silver streams that shut the house in a prison of shining bars. Andrea looked out at it, bored to nausea, then paced the floor with a blanket around her shoulders. Once she started out onto the landing but, imagining footsteps, quickly retreated. She hadn't seen the punk now for several days but the sweet smell of marijuana and sound of rock music kept her always aware of his proximity, and every time she thought of him striking her, her cheek stung and she simmered with loathing. Time and imagination embellished his evil so that her hatred intensified at the same pace as her fondness for the pregnant girl. Surely that poor soul was his victim also, forced to accept her situation by who knows what outrageous threats.

The rain thundered relentlessly. Depression weighed on Andrea like a bad dream. The world had forgotten her. She envisioned her son, the men and women she worked with, all the people she knew, those who had been at the funeral, going about their daily affairs without giving her a thought. They might never know. But worse than anything else—she'd lost herself. Where was Andrea James? Not that makeup free, limp-haired person she sometimes caught glimpses of in the mirror. She looked down at her chipped nail polish and, overwhelmed by hopelessness, pushed her face into the pillow, willing it to smother her.

She didn't try to speak to the old man when he came, just took the food and ate automatically, then without washing curled up in bed. Tears trailed across her face. "But I was always alone," the sensible one told the child inside her. But the child replied, "There was Robert. Remember, just last year when the car broke down near San Jose? One phone call and he came fifty miles to bring you home? He was always there when you needed him. If he were alive now he'd find you. If he were alive I wouldn't be here at all!" thought Andrea. "Everything is your fault. You shouldn't have left. Oh Robert!" She found herself sitting up, reaching toward nothing, and fell back with a heavy thud.

CHAPTER SIXTEEN

More rain made the next day a continuation of endless night. She huddled in bed until long after the knock sounded on her door so when she collected her breakfast the porridge was glutinous and the tea cold. She left it untouched and sat unwashed and uncombed at the closed window, watching dark streaks flail across the moor to lash against the house. Trees bent and swayed. Branches rasped across the slate roof. She didn't bother to turn on the light. She didn't even think anymore.

By late afternoon the rain had stopped but clouds broiled high and the wind still gusted. When dinner came Andrea exchanged it with the uneaten breakfast and without a word returned listlessly to her chair. She didn't bother to close the door, and it was a few minutes before the footsteps left. She paid no attention, just set the tray down and leaned her head back, dozing where she was. The soup grew cold. A moon glinted and disappeared to glimmer again moments later.

Befuddled with sleep, Andrea awoke aware that something had disturbed her. The world slept. There... that faint scratching. The hairs on her neck rose, then she recognized the tap of the old man. Now? Why? After a moment's hesitation she struggled from the chair and freed herself from the blanket. The tap was repeated, scarcely audible, almost as though the owl that hooted softly outside had brushed the wood with its wings. She put her hand on the latch and pulled, but before she had the door half open a bundle was thrust toward her. "Put 'em on," was the whispered command.

"What…?" She faintly made out a pair of trousers and a heavy black sweater. Wellington boots and heavy socks were placed in front of her. "Put 'em on!" the voice growled.

"Why…?"

"You'll look right daft on the moor in those clothes you've got."

"The moor?" Bodies in hidden graves. They were going to kill her. "Is he going?"

"Stop gabbin' and get dressed or the night'll be gone and you'll miss your chance."

My God, the old gaffer's going to help me get away! Galvanized into action Andrea tussled herself into the clothes. They were too big and not very clean but so long as they got her out of here… "I'm ready."

"Hush then." He beckoned her to follow and she tried desperately to be quiet in her clumsy footwear. Twice the man put his finger to his lips as Andrea started down the dark stairwell. On the small landing she paused, gathering courage to traverse that area that could cost her Robert's ashes and perhaps her own life.

The hand beckoned and, shifting all responsibility onto him, she plunged down. At the bottom she paused and looked toward the kitchen but the door was closed and no sound came from behind it. The punk must be away. Still her mouth was dry and it seemed a miracle when they stepped out safely into the night.

No time was allowed to relish the moment, her rescuer had already disappeared around the corner of the house and she hurried to catch up, past her car and the vegetable garden to a small iron gate set between two stone posts. Nearby a shed with a round eye of a window lurked behind some conifers. The man waited, holding the way open, and the moon made it easy to see they were about to enter the field she saw from her window. But Andrea had noticed something else and she stiffened with dismay.

"C'mon. What's up?"

"You've not got Robert's ashes. Where are they?"

"Where t'lad put 'em, I s'pose."

"But I can't leave without them."

"Course you can't. I wouldn't have brung you otherwise."

"You mean you're not helping me escape?"

"Nay, woman, I couldn't do that. It's just—I can't abide seein' any live thing cooped up, and you lookin' as peaked as you did this evenin'…"

Andrea stood, weak with disappointment, angry, cheated—and confused.

"Run off, mind, and the lad, Newt, will throw your husband on the rubbish heap. Me too, I don't doubt. Don't think he won't." He studied her face, awaiting her reaction.

What could she do? She sighed and shrugged. At least she was outside.

The man turned and began to move away.

Hesitantly Andrea followed. It was too dark—already he was just a faint shape. She looked around. So much space. The wind hurled warnings and unseen things moved in the grass… no place to be alone. She broke into a trot and was surprised to find he hadn't gone far at all.

Now she stayed close, following on the narrow path that crossed the field. It grew steeper. Andrea looked with dread at the hill ahead that appeared to rise into black nothingness. Her heart already thumped so she could hear little else. "You can't expect me to walk up that!" She reached out to grasp the jacket ahead of her, but stopped before she touched it. "I can't possibly."

He faced her, a tall and commanding stranger under the moonlight. "No?"

"It's too steep… it's dark, and I'm not young…"

Was that shine in his eyes contempt or amusement? "You'll soon see right enough, and what's age to do with owt lest you let it? Come if you wish, stay if you will. Tis nowt to me."

Tears filled Andrea's eyes and throat as she watched him

stride away up the now rough track, climbing effortlessly, and dissolving into the night. Then suddenly she was angry. "Damn you," she muttered. Then louder, "Damn you!" On the strength of her fury she hastened after him, stumbling over tussocks and panicked by each scattering of ghostly, startled sheep which seemed bunched at every turn. She continued while her muscles and lungs burned and the night became a kaleidoscope of confusion and discomfort, filled with the rasp of her own breathing.

Finally she stopped and doubled over, unable to take another step. Even her brain was numb. In time, when her breath eased and the pain subsided, she straightened and, as she inhaled a deep reviving gulp of air, she saw Robert silhouetted on the crown of the hill against the black sky. Involuntarily she called his name and ran toward him.

The shape beckoned and began to move away. "Robert!" Andrea called again, forcing herself to go faster. "Please wait," she pleaded under her breath. "Please. Please." Moonlight limned the white beard of the man who waited for her and she stopped in her tracks, bewildered. "Dear God! I must be mad!" she thought. "What was I thinking? Robert's dead—ashes in a box. Even if it were his ghost, it's not me he'd be beckoning to. This is Lesley's ground. It's her he'd come for, not me." Like a cancer, pain blossomed, fresh but not new. She recognized the same agony she had crushed into dormancy so many years before, cutting like a razor, making her bleed into weakness that almost made her collapse. Yet for one sweet moment she had felt such joy.

The internal tumult eased. The wind sighed... a stream chuckled... a lamb called tremulously. And all the while the man in front of her waited, quietly watching until she caught up.

He gave a small grunt and they started on again with Andrea trudging behind. He'd probably not heard her, he was old and perhaps a bit deaf. But, even as she thought this, she marveled at his upright figure and the way his stride devoured the ground with all the power and spring attributed to youth.

Minutes passed and although they travelled more slowly than before, she began wheezing again. She struggled on until the pain in her calves became unbearable, then she sank onto a rock. "Please, I've got to rest," she gasped, in a humbler tone than she would have thought possible.

The old man gave no acknowledgement other than to stop and look down into the valley from which they had just climbed.

It was sheltered here, close to the ground; an island of calm. Andrea massaged her legs, then studied her companion. His starlit face was peaceful and closed on his own thoughts. "Why, he's really quite beautiful," she thought. The beard gave gentleness and wisdom to a long aquiline face and his eyes, set deep in dark hollows, seemed unutterably sad. "He could be a gypsy," she thought. "Or a hippy, with that long hair. But it's the way he carries himself... he looks so damn proud. As though he owns all this wild land." Funny how up until now she'd always thought him ancient and frail. The climb had been effortless for him... "I must have been mistaken, he isn't old at all," she thought.

What was he listening to so intently? She wanted to ask, but something about him demanded silence. Long ago she and Robert had shared moments where no words were needed, but then she had begun to realize he was probably thinking of Lesley so began a campaign of constant chatter to keep him with her. Later she had either avoided such situations or someone had been with them.

She looked down to where she could make out the vague shapes of trees and houses where the village clustered out of the wind, then up to the opposite ridge where moor stretched into a nighttime of space. Andrea shivered at the wonderful, frightening, magnitude of it. Time passed. She relaxed. The wind gusted and whistled between the stones of a nearby wall and she brushed hair from her eyes in a gesture once habitual to the girl she had been. Her hair had been long and dark then... she had dreamed of roaming over such a place as this...

"Damn!" She flung a pebble she hadn't known she'd held and it clattered on others.

The man turned inquiringly toward her.

"It's too late," she said bitterly, not really to him. "I used to imagine myself roaming all over this country. Now I get here I can barely cross one damn field!"

"You're just soft, you'll soon toughen up." The words, an underbreath to the wind, sounded like an echo from long ago. Rob had taken her hiking up Mount Tamalpais soon after Leslie was born. She'd puffed like a steam engine. "We'll soon toughen you up," Rob had laughed, pulling her by the hand and kissing her on the nose.

Andrea had imagined the way Lesley would have bounded along beside him and was ashamed.

She had never gone again. Had produced one excuse after another… he had loved hiking… perhaps their son had gone with him sometimes.

She wished this man cared enough to kiss her on the nose… "Andrea, whatever are you thinking!" But she smiled as she scolded herself.

"Are you ready to move on?" he said.

Andrea got to her feet hoping that "on" meant back down, and yet in a way she didn't want to leave. "What's your name? What should I call you?"

"Pops. Most folks call me Pops now. I was called Mathew."

Andrea had moved closer to hear him over the wind which now attacked her ears. She could smell him, a warm distillation of heather, peat and sheep, and she knew she would never forget it. Pops? That may suit the man in the house but not this one. She could never call him that. "Have you always lived here?"

"Off and on."

A cloud unveiled the moon. Andrea looked down at herself and laughed. "God, just look at me!"

He made no reply and she wished she hadn't said it. Vanity had no place here.

Silence made them part of the scenery, the complaint of the lamb continuing background.

"Mathew?"

"Aye?"

"I've heard there's an interesting church in Starwell. Where is it?"

"Religious are you? Look to the right end of the village. If you've sharp eyes you maybe can make out the steeple."

Andrea couldn't see it but she imagined the grave that marked the end of her journey. A church began it and a church must end it. Seldom since that pact with her gentle God had turned sour and made her suffer so, had she attended a service. Only Leslie's christening, a few weddings and funerals. She had almost learned to hate Him.

Those eyes were watching her again, dark and piercing from under the shadow of his brow as though he could read her mind.

"I can't see anything," she muttered. "I suppose you can?"

"I don't need to look, Lass. I can see everything hereabouts with my eyes closed."

"But you can't see inside my head," Andrea thought, as she followed him along beside a wall. She glanced back for one last look to where the church must be and thought how, if things had gone as planned, Robert's ashes would be on the grave now and it would all be over. She would be on her way home, starting her new life devoid of both Robert, God and Lesley. She stopped. What a bleak thought! It didn't pay to think too much. "Why do you stay with that crazy boy?" The question blurted out on its own.

"Because..." He had stopped too but he looked intently off into the darkness. "Folks," he said softly, "can get in a bind, y'know. Like you wi' them ashes."

He strode away from her.

"Mathew?"

He was almost invisible already.

"Mathew!"

She thought she heard him whisper, "Wait." Then a cloud took away the moon and he was gone.

Andrea waited, every nerve taut. Had he really said anything or was it just the wind moaning through the grass? How had she thought it quiet? And that lamb was still shrilly bleating. She waited. Now there was only the wind. She tasted blood from where she chewed the inside of her lip. He'd been gone a long time… what if he didn't return? Suddenly it hit her. "Oh my God, of course, that was it. He meant to desert me! Knew I'd try to get back for Robert's sake, but be late and get caught. That punk'll kill me!" Fear blinded her with tears and she brushed them away, frantically searching the night but seeing nothing. "Damn, damn. What an idiot I was, thinking he cared about me. Why on earth should he, he never uttered a single civil word to me before. The old guy was fed up with bringing me food and having to watch out for me all the time. I'm the damn bind he meant! Of course he wants to get rid of me. And to think I was fool enough to imagine there was something special about him." A village clock tolled one. Or was it one? Maybe it was half past something, or two or three with the other sounds blown away! Andrea found herself turning in small circles. "Calm down," she scolded, facing the valley. "I must find my way there quickly, sneak in and thwart the old devil. If only the moon would come out so I could see…"

CHAPTER SEVENTEEN

Andrea started along what she hoped was a trail. Hurry. Run! A rut brought her to her knees. She smelled damp earth—felt it under her fingernails. Tasted salt. Damn! Damn! Scrambling up she fought to get her bearings but mist shrouded the valley, camouflaging the dark shapes of landmark trees that hid the house she must reach before it was too late. She sensed the approach of dawn and forced herself to begin again.

Oh!"

She almost collided with the figure that blocked her way. Silver beard glinted.

"Oh." Surprise left her breathless so she could only stare, then she was flooded with relief. Mathew had not betrayed her!

"Eh, lass, couldn't you bide a minute? You'll get yoursel' lost wanderin' about on yer own. Have ye no patience?"

An abbreviated bleat drew attention to the bundle in his arms, and looking closely she saw a lamb wrapped in his coat.

"Lost. Got through t'wall. Couldn't get back to 'is mum." More material was pulled protectively around the shivering creature. "We'll find 'er on the way down."

Andrea reached out to touch the hard little head, and stroked the big ears while the lamb raised its black nose and took her finger in its mouth trying to suckle. "Oh, baby, you silly little guy, did you go and lose yourself?" She put her face close to his and smelled the sweet milky breath, hiding tears that insisted on filling her throat. What was the matter with her? She felt so weak, so ready to weep instead of getting on with things as she used to. Her finger was dropped impatiently and the mouth opened in a trilling call to be answered by another, stronger and deeper.

"Mum." Mathew lowered the lamb gently to the ground where it turned toward the ewe which emerged from the night all ears and maternal panic. A moment's hesitation and the youngster broke into a staggering run until the two ghosts melded and disappeared.

"Come," said Mathew heading down the hill at a different angle to that which Andrea had been about to take.

Reluctantly she dragged her eyes from now empty space and began to follow.

"You mustn't wander by yersel' out here. You were heading for a nasty bit of bog."

"And how was I to know you'd ever come back?" Andrea snapped.

Mathew stopped and looked at her. He didn't say anything— just looked. Then he sighed and strode on.

They took their muddy boots off outside and, carrying them, crept into the house. Nothing stirred. Mathew stood aside to let Andrea go upstairs and when she turned to whisper good night he was gone.

Her room, when she turned on the light, was welcoming and familiar, and as she sat on the edge of the bed thinking over all that had happened that night, one hand rose to her nose bringing remnants of the lamb's sweetly acrid scent. She smiled, then clasped both hands tightly together, squeezing them with excitement, as she thought about the man on the moor. A man who held lambs close to his heart to keep them warm. Someone who would look after her too… perhaps! She stuffed the boots well under the bed out of sight and as she pulled the turtleneck over her head she paused, attention caught by the tousle haired woman with shining eyes who looked back at her from the mirror. Was that really her? A stranger, but so very familiar. Something about her reflection puzzled her, then scared her so she pressed the light switch and finished undressing in the dark.

Next morning the stiffness in her legs was a blessing as it alone proved that her outing hadn't been a dream. The birds sang their same songs, the moor looked as unattainable as ever and, after his usual soft knock, the old man stood as always, mutely offering her tray, eyes down. Andrea stopped on the indrawn breath of her aborted welcome. Could this be the same person who strode so boldly ahead of her only hours before? She wanted desperately to say something but didn't, terrified that the eyes would look at her blankly, denying the whole night's adventure. Confused and hurt she watched him shuffle away. But it had happened! Quickly she put the tray down, and kneeled beside the bed. Reaching under it she triumphantly pulled out the boots and broke off a chunk of still wet mud which she rubbed between her fingers. It's dank smell took her back... "Yes", she whispered, "Whatever else happens, I know I was there." She rehid the boots and opened the wardrobe door. The heavy sweater and trousers were where she'd hung them and as she held the rough sleeve against her cheek she envisioned the figure that had evoked such deep feelings the night before and again felt pain from the morning's rebuff. She so badly wanted him to like her. But why should he? He had taken her out of kindness and she had only been unpleasant in return. With a flood of shame Andrea remembered her whining complaints. Saw again his disappointment after she'd accused him of deserting her. She, who envied that small lamb for being held so protectively, hadn't even thanked him... "Oh God," she thought, "He'll probably never take me again."

Dejectedly she ate the porridge. There seemed more than usual. Through the window she saw blue sky with puffs of white cloud, and sunshine that seemed apologetic for its two days' absence. Across the field and up the hill she traced a trail. Was that the stone where they'd rested? It seemed very distant but she was sure it was. "I was there," she whispered to the picture of Lesley. "I walked all that way—and I touched a lamb." She said it proudly, like a girl who has just lost her virginity and next day feels the triumph of joining her more

97

worldly sisters on a new level of experience. "And I will go again," she said, defiantly.

Was Lesley laughing at her?

Maybe Mathew wasn't angry at all. Perhaps he knew that the Mohawk haired monster was listening at the foot of the stairs. He was being careful not to give them away. That was probably it!

Andrea's cloud of gloom dissolved in the flick of a gnat's wing and she inspected her room with new eyes, recalling the welcoming feel of it on her return last night. What pretty wallpaper! Her fingers traced one grouping of tiny blue flowers—they almost matched the blue of the mat on the dark floorboards. Everything was just a little bit crooked, as though the builder had measured by feel rather than plans and rulers. She liked that. In modern California she'd have sued over such workmanship, but here it added character. She touched the door frame. Who had made it? What had his life been like so long ago? And the mirror... what reflections had it captured supposing it had been here during the cottage's three centuries. All the women and all their days. Andrea could almost see them. Old and wrinkled, middle-aged, smiling and tearful, and the young girls who could never have imagined cars, or planes. Had they heard rumors of America and thought of it as we think of the moon? How strange to be so alive then—only to be forgotten now. A ghost in a mirror. Andrea looked into her own questioning grey eyes. Was she also now held forever deep in that wavy glass? If she concentrated hard enough could she go beyond the looking glass and meet all those who had once looked out?

She pulled away with difficulty, almost as though she had been half way there. Drawing a deep breath she turned to look again around the four walls. Home. It would be nice to hang some pictures, maybe like the one on the stairs. For a moment she was thoughtful, perhaps sometime when she was feeling brave she could take it; but for now she could at least make the bed.

After completing that, she took out one of her silk scarves and used it as a duster, then opened the dresser drawers in preparation for the contents of her suitcase. They were all empty except for the bottom one in which lay a piece of needlepoint. Andrea held it up to the light. Against a green background a black and white collie looked adoringly at a young farm boy who leaned against a gate. Matt and His Dog was the title sewn underneath. It must have taken someone a long time to put in all those tiny stitches. She peered closely at the boy's face. He seemed to be looking longingly into the distance while one hand reached affectionately toward his pet. Whoever made this knew Matt and loved him. His mother perhaps? Andrea found two pins in her sewing kit and pinned her find to the wall above her bed. She stood back and admired it. The room was really hers now. It really was! No one else ever came here. She could do anything she liked. Make the bed or not. Dress or not. Her captivity had brought freedom. Excitedly she placed her belongings in the drawers and slid the suitcase under the bed with the boots. Now flowers. She looked around for a vase— that bottle of cologne in her makeup bag would do. She found it and ran to the bathroom where she poured its contents down the drain. Ugh! Her nose wrinkled. How could she ever have worn such stuff?

After several vigorous rinsings she half filled the bottle with water and returned to her room. Two rosebuds were just within reach of her window, and she snipped them with nail scissors. They eked the smallest amount of delicious fragrance and Andrea closed her eyes, holding them close to her nose for a moment before squeezing the stems through the narrow neck of the new vase and setting them on the dresser. Their redness glowed, intensifying her delight, and she was bemused to realize she was as happy today as she had been miserable yesterday.

On impulse she picked up pen and paper from the dressing table, dragged the chair close to the window and began to write, spilling out her feelings of the morning, describing her room, and then last night. Her pen hovered as she thought back, half smiling. Focusing again she noticed the salutation she had begun with. My dear Robert... how strange... she hadn't thought of sharing any experience with him for many years... now he was gone... how sad. He felt closer here. It really had looked like him out there on the moor... He had been wonderful when she first knew him. Young and passionate and loving. Maybe she could forget what followed and just pretend... for a little while. What harm could it do? He couldn't hurt her anymore and she needn't even worry about the damned ashes. Andrea bent her head and began again to write about the excitement of the wind, the rough, honest abrasiveness of stone... and the strong hands that had held the shivering lamb so very gently. Robert's hands would have been like that...

A strange off-key humming interrupted her, and removing the end of the pen from her lips Andrea leaned forward to look out the window. The girl was in the garden again. It had been a long two days. As the young woman began to work with the hoe Andrea frowned. Something was wrong. The usual energy was missing. She rested too often, massaging her back, and the sound she made was more like that of an angry bee. Usually her feyness added more color to the garden but today she seemed drained, a flower turned toadstool. Even her long fingers seemed weak and pallid. The only lively thing about her was the blue ribbon that fluttered from her braid. Andrea frowned. Was the girl eating properly? Did she ever go to a doctor? So much could happen to an expectant mother...

"Rowan, get inside. Tha' looks proper poorly."

Andrea shrank back as the half-shaven head of the punk came into view below, and remembrance of that hand smashing into her cheek made her stomach squirm and her skin go cold. She hadn't seen him since then. He had just been a presence to be avoided. Now she stared with fascination, as she would at a reptile, because this time his attention was not on her.

From this vantage point he looked small, but his bare arms were all muscle and his stride long as he stalked toward the girl and wrested the hoe from her hands. "Get inside."

She wiped a muddy hand on her shirt and began to sob. "Oh, Newt, I look awful! I feel awful! Let me go, Newt, please let me go!"

Such pleading. Andrea's heart went out to her.

"You'll go nowheres but in by yon fire. And take off yer shoes, they're reet mucky."

"You're always telling me what to do!" Two spots of color inflamed the girl's cheeks. "I'm tired of you ordering me about! If I want to come out here I will. There's nowt else to do in this beastly place! I hate you!" Her voice grew louder and shriller, shrieking, raising the hairs on Andrea's neck. Careful, child. Be careful! Don't get him angry, you know he's crazy! How she longed to rush down to help... persuade him to agree to the girl's plea... let her go... but she couldn't even help herself.

The cat scurried from one hiding place to another.

"There's plenty to do inside. Get in and close the door." The punk's tones were cold and measured.

"You're a mean, nasty pig." Rowan walked up to Newt and swung at him.

"Oh no!" Andrea stiffened, heart thumping. Surely he'd kill her!

But the punk had caught Rowan's arm before the blow landed.

The two figures stood like statues, glaring at each other, then he slowly lowered her hand.

"Inside," he commanded.

The girl spun around and darted for the door, but even before she had disappeared Andrea again heard that strange tune bubbling from her lips, and it left her feeling oddly bewildered, her anger an empty gust of wind.

In her concern she had stepped into plain view to anyone looking upward and now she hastily backed behind the curtain where, trembling with emotion, she admired the brave girl's stand and pitied her for living with that inhuman tyrant. Thank God he never came upstairs. Poor Rowan. Poor little thing.

Pretty name, Rowan. Weird name, Newt!

Andrea peeked out. At first she thought the punk had gone, but no, there he was crouching, scratching with a stick in the dirt and staring into space. He sure looked stupid in that T-shirt with the arms torn off and ripped jeans. Funny how his sort never felt the cold. Scrawny from taking dope instead of food— all sinew and insolence. Her inspection reached his face. Not really all that ugly. In spite of the dense, angry eyebrows, crooked nose and thick lips there was something compelling there. If he'd wipe off that stupid makeup and stop shaving his head so he looked like a parakeet. But he was evil—and crazy— imprisoning people like herself and Rowan and maybe Mathew? What hold did he have over them? Unlike her they could walk away. Why didn't they? Was it fear? The girl's pregnancy perhaps?

Andrea jerked back. The object of her inspection had suddenly straightened and flung a weed with its clump of earth violently against a tree. As Andrea watched, his face twisted with some strong emotion, then all at once he looked up, and their eyes locked. For a long moment they seemed unable to break away, then the old sneer formed, he gave her the finger and stalked back into the house.

Andrea stayed at the window breathing hard, listening for his footsteps on the stairs, expecting all that violence to come up to punish her. Had that clump of earth that he'd smashed into the tree been a skull in his own mind? Killing would come easily to him. Andrea shuddered.

When she finally realized he wasn't coming she closed the window and went back to her chair and writing pad, but the words wouldn't come anymore. Instead she found a pencil and began to sketch. She had taken art classes in college and been quite good, now she once again became involved and the only sound in the room was that of bold strokes used to portray a dark, tangled moor with walls running across it like chains, and streaks of rain dashing from angry clouds. Her pencil lead snapped, and just then the mealtime tap sounded on her door.

She answered eagerly, sure there'd be a sign that Mathew would come for her later, some slight hint in his demeanor, a note, even a raised eyebrow; but there was nothing. He handed over her food, not holding the tray an instant longer than was necessary, then left without a breath of recognition. Without a wisp of hope. He didn't give a damn! Nobody did! Andrea banged the tray down so soup spilled and a slice of bread slipped off its plate to soak up the soggy stain. Then she sobbed, tearlessly, so her chest and throat ached.

And yet she waited. She couldn't help herself. Her eyes kept straying to the fading line of heather against sky, hope like a trapped bird against her ribs.

When at last it was completely dark, she arose like a sleepwalker and put on the old clothes, setting the boots ready to climb into. Again she sat down. He will come. He will come. A sound from below broke through her internal chant and when she opened her door a babble of voices announced arrivals downstairs. The punk welcomed someone and led the way into the kitchen. Andrea returned to her chair and sat, tense, hearing surges of loud talk, then smelling marijuana. Surely they'd leave soon. There was no hope of Mathew coming while they were here. Please leave, she whispered. Then the music began—loud, crashing rock. One tune over and over, sometimes stopping abruptly in the middle of a phrase, only to begin again with more gusto and thunder, on into the next crashing fuselage of musical weaponry to keep her prisoner. She thought it would never end, while outside the night waited, cool and unperturbed.

"Why in hell don't they go?" she blurted, and switching on the light, went over to look at Lesley's face. A small, amused smile played about the mouth.

"What are you looking so smug for anyway? You've meddled about in the rest of my life, it wouldn't hurt you to do something now. And let me tell you, if you ever want Robert you'd better do something about it, I've done my best."

Lesley still smiled and the errant thought that perhaps she

did not want Robert washed once around Andrea's mind and was flung aside.

She lay back on the bed staring at the ceiling light. Long ago, one night in the first few weeks of their acquaintanceship, she'd waited like this for Robert. He was late and she began to think he never would come; had decided to never see her again. But finally he arrived, full of apologies and explaining how his father had called and kept him talking. They were going to a movie she'd chosen that had been filmed in Yorkshire, and they almost ran the few blocks to the theater. God, she'd been so proud to have him beside her! Had looked at other girls and pitied them and their humdrum lives, dating boring men with no real romance in their souls. It was then that she'd sworn never to give Robert up and she knew she could keep him by loving what he loved most and keeping it alive for him. No one else would ever be able to do that like she could.

He'd taken her hand in the movie while a gale blew across the moors and the beautiful woman searched for her lover.

That was the first night he made love to her, back in her rented room, terrified the landlady would hear them. He'd said wonderful things, his face flushed with passion and his eyes on fire. During sex with other men Andrea's mind had always remained active, judging each move, thinking about timing, too soon, too late, too fast, too slow, was her toe going to cramp, would he want her to do this or that... but with Robert she thought of nothing at all and when it was over and they lay, glued together by sweat, it was like returning from a magical journey. Oh, my God, she thought, you are wonderful!

A shout from downstairs brought Andrea upright. The music had stopped. Someone laughed loudly. Nervously, Andrea pushed the chair against the door handle and turned out the light. Footsteps sounded on the stair. Drunken mumbling. She hunkered at the head of the bed pulling the blanket around her. What if they came in? Maybe that's what happened to Rowan.

"The bloody door's locked."

Someone had tried the room across the hall.

"Nay, the loo's down at the end, but I think it's broke. They use the one out back of the pantry." That was a woman's voice.

"What's in these other rooms?"

Andrea leapt silently to the door and held the latch firm against the hand that tried to raise it.

"Eh, Lads, coom down. Newt keeps this out of bounds like. Lights might get seen in t' village." It was Mathew.

"Oh, Aye."

Footsteps receded.

Andrea released the breath she unconsciously held. Thank goodness!

But those people might have rescued her! She'd only assumed they were the enemy. Had Mathew just saved her or made sure she stayed prisoner? She didn't know anything anymore. She banged her head against the old boards, hands still pressing the door closed, and again began to cry.

CHAPTER EIGHTEEN

She slept in those old clothes then refused to answer the knock when Mathew brought breakfast. She didn't want him to guess her disappointment. Mathew, the jailer. Mathew her only hope. Which was he?

She remembered him as he had been up on the hill and felt she would die if she couldn't go with him again. "Oh, Mathew, please don't leave me shut up here forever. Please care about me." Except for the tray holding its oatmeal and a boiled egg, the hallway was empty when she looked out.

That eleventh day seemed an eternity. She thought she'd go crazy with boredom, and anxiety tied knots in her stomach so she couldn't even pretend to find something to do. The sun shone but no one came into the garden, except the cat who prowled like a small tiger among the cabbages. Andrea worried about Rowan, imagining all the things that could go wrong in pregnancy.

Perhaps if she leaned out she'd hear some sound from the kitchen, but just as she put her elbows on the sill the girl dashed out, shouting to the cat, "There you are!"

Andrea jumped back, cracking her head on the window frame, and as she rubbed the pain Rowan scooped up her pet and darted back inside.

"Damn it! Stay out, at least for a little while!" Andrea muttered.

A blackbird flew down and scratched under the elder bush where the cat had lain and other birds twittered and swooped. One carrying a beak full of straw flew into the larch behind the shed. It was nesting time.

Andrea got a piece of paper and sketched a rolling skyline, then she covered the rest of the page with the name Mathew, over and over, making the M and the W big and swirly.

She scarcely noticed the guitar music when it began. It was as though it was her own mind searching for a tune, then it grew louder, more assured, and she sat back to listen. A young male voice began to sing, rousing and defiant, and beneath—like an echo—another—the girl's. Andrea sat on the window sill, legs swinging in rhythm.

The music stopped, there was laughter, and the outside kitchen door banged shut.

Andrea sat on in the stillness. Evening approached and with it the rank odor of disappointment. She closed the window and made herself go to bed where she lay sleepless with a small ache in her chest.

Mathew came.

At first Andrea couldn't believe it when he knocked, then she jumped up muttering, "Thank God, Thank God", as she scrambled into her clothes. Soon she was following him downstairs and out into the garden where she looked up into the dark sky, loving the exuberant wind.

Not once did she look back at the shadowy house. This time she hurried through the iron gate and up the hill, denying any ache in her calves or the rasping pain of her lungs. Nothing mattered but that she was free, and with him. Her energy began to flag by the time they reached the first stile but she refused to ask for a moment's rest and struggled onward, cursing herself for being tired. If only she could shake off this clumsy body. If only she could move like the man ahead of her... see in the dark as he could. Awakened sheep didn't lumber away from him, he was only a passing breeze to them. But from her... she was like an elephant.

"Are ye alright?"

He stopped and Andrea, acutely aware of her wheezing, lied,

"I'm fine."

"Look."

The hill dropped away to their left and Andrea looked down over shades of grey to where the glint of a river snaked through a dark valley. Two sparks moved near it. Headlights. She watched them slide along next to the serpent then turn toward it and disappear. Swallowed. Close by wind whished through grass and now and again small high-pitched sounds came from birds or small animals.

She turned, about to ask the river's name, but the words died on her lips as she realized Mathew was intent on listening. She listened too but heard nothing unusual. Again her gaze caressed that fierce, noble profile and, remembering how gentle he could be, she thought how different he was to other men. He was a being from another world, with his strange, spare way of speaking and proud easy carriage.

"Why do you live with that creature called Newt? Who are they, he and the girl?" As soon as the words escaped her mouth she could have kicked herself, and Mathew's reaction was no surprise as he turned his back and strode on up the trail.

She watched him, angry, refusing to follow. After all where was the law against asking a question? He didn't look back and eventually she had to give in and close the gap, although she made sure to leave it wide enough for him to notice. But he didn't and she struggled along feeling miserable and sorry for herself. It wasn't fair! The whole damn thing wasn't fair! Deep inside, Andrea was amused to see herself reduced to a six year old. She remembered her mother walking away down a busy sidewalk while she, the recalcitrant child who had refused to leave some tempting chocolates in a store window, straggled along behind calling in increasingly desperate tones, "Wait for me! Wait for me!"

"You're doing reet well tonight. D'you feel better?"

She hadn't noticed Mathew dropping back beside her for he, like her mother, had finally waited. Gratitude welled in Andrea as she nodded but when she searched for his eyes she found nothing but darkness.

"What name am I to call you, lass?"

"My name's Andrea."

"Well, Andy, it's time we got home."

Andy. It was a long time since anyone had called her that.

Now she followed closely. The footing seemed easy and she was able to look around, sniffing the rich smells of bracken and peat and sheep.

The garden gate came all too soon and Andrea gave one long look backward before going through.

"Well done," Mathew murmured as they entered the house, and she managed to whisper a heartfelt thanks before they parted at the foot of the stairs.

"Well done." Those words of praise made her unbelievably happy and she repeated them often during the next day. They fanned a spark in her that glowed like an awakened coal in an abandoned hearth and as she remembered the gentleness in that soft voice, her spirit leapt and she looked up at the skyline and swore that she would make him admire her—and like her, maybe even love her.

"Andy, that's crazy," she thought, but she didn't care, she felt as happy and excited as when she'd first met Robert so long ago. The voice of reason put up faint argument. "He's old." "Not really, I don't think so really." "He's your jailer." "But he feeds me and takes me onto his moor."

Besides there was no one to know, and it felt so good to care about someone, to have that thrill of long forgotten expectation... why not?

Rowan entered the garden and began to work, cumbersome, but for the dancing green ribbon that fluttered from her braid. "Dear beautiful Rowan," Andrea thought, settling into her usual watching place. "You don't know it but I love you too." A small robin alighted surprisingly close on a branch near the girl who, smiling, reached out her right hand. The bird fluttered to it, balanced on the inviting thumb and cocked its glistening eye. The moment stayed frozen, magic, fitting Andrea's mood.

Suddenly Rowan's other hand arose in a lightening swipe. With shrill tweet and panicked beating of wings the bird only just escaped.

Andrea gasped. The malice in that blow…! What happened!

Already, as though the ugly moment had never happened, Rowan was petting the cat that circled and purred around her legs, chattering and cooing to it. Had the bird pecked her, causing that vicious response? It hadn't seemed to.

A shiver went through Andrea. "Like someone walking on my grave," she thought. "There must have been some reason I couldn't see, Rowan would never hurt anything."

Meanwhile the girl had picked up the hoe and recommenced work among the weeds and vegetables and marigolds. Andrea thrust what had happened out of her mind and became so involved she could almost feel the old hoe's smooth wooden handle against her own fingers, the tensing of her own muscles at each chop. She wasn't close enough to see if worms wriggled in the newly turned soil but she was sure they did—and it must smell good.

Tendrils of Rowan's hair escaped its plait to halo her head with gold and Andrea imagined herself brushing that hair and winding it, smooth strand over strand over strand, and then stroking away the frown that periodically wrinkled the pale brow. "I could tell her not to be afraid of having the baby. I'll be here to help." If she and Robert had had a daughter she'd be about this age… how hard it was not to call out. Just a hello. A little wave. But she mustn't. That tranquil garden world would surely vanish like the rainbow in a punctured soap bubble if she intruded. But she could dream… there was no harm in that. And it was even more like a dream because however much Rowan worked there were never any perceivable results. The place was little better than a jungle for all the girl's hoeing and weeding, as though a fecundity of plant life was forever crowding beneath the ground, clamoring for the chance to spring into sunlight. But the garden was nice this way and the exercise was good for the soon-to-be mother. Yet a whisper of disquiet had marred the perfect afternoon.

Andrea left to go to the bathroom and when she reentered her room a hullabaloo outside brought her rushing to her place behind the lace curtain.

The girl stood below, hands on hips, facing the kitchen door, her face red and screwed up with rage. "Why don't you let me go?" She screamed. "You don't own me. You don't, you don't, you don't!" She stamped her feet and waved the rake like a weapon.

"I told you yesterday you'll stay here and like it," came Newt's voice.

"Your friend said I should go. You heard him. I want to, Newt, I truly do." A wheedling tone arose. "Please, let me! I know the way."

Immediately Newt was out, grasping her shoulders and shaking them. "And you'll bloody well forget it!" He bellowed.

Rowan cried. Screaming harsh, staccato gasps. "You don't give me enough to eat. There's nothing to do." Her arms dropped to her sides and the hoe clattered to the ground.

She was the picture of despair. "Oh child, child," Andrea whispered, "Be patient. Enjoy your secret world. Please. When I go I will take you, and you will be my daughter."

"I hate it all. I hate you. I wish you were dead! Let me go!" Fury had taken over, so consuming that even Andrea cowered.

The punk stepped back, rubbing his hands. "Shut up, Rowan! I'll get more food, you'll see, but I'll not let you go. Never will I do that, lass, never."

"Work your own bloody garden!" Rowan stormed into the house with Newt following.

The stage was empty. Andrea trembled. As moments passed she began to see Rowan's outburst as a splendid rage! This was the second time the girl had confronted their jailer, and he'd actually backed down... been humbled. "If only you knew how proud I am of you."

The punk reappeared. Alone. Something was different about him. Andrea had been so intent on Rowan she hadn't noticed before but it was that awful makeup, he wasn't wearing it! It had never occurred to her that he must wash sometime—that the stuff actually came off. Not that she could see his face very well from this angle but his usually arrogant row of hair now flopped sideways, covering one eye, and his shoulders slumped as though under an enormous burden. Well, serve the little bastard right! She followed his progress across the garden and behind the tool shed. There he leaned his forehead against the boards and put both hands to his face. As if he were crying! Andrea closed her eyes, shutting out the unlikely sight, and instead saw her own son Leslie, eyes red from weeping. She had been shocked to find him this way but had pretended not to notice and he had never told her what troubled him. She hadn't pressed it. Hadn't wanted to hear of loneliness.

Of course there was no similarity between Leslie and this monster.

Andrea opened her eyes.

The boy had straightened and now turned his face skyward, tightening his fists at his sides. He squared his shoulders, spat, and swaggered back through the garden and into the house.

Andrea pulled her bed completely apart and remade it, concentrating on removing each wrinkle and making each corner perfect. Then she washed her hair in cold water in the small bathroom basin and as she toweled it dry she paused, still shivering, and sniffed. A smile twitched her lip corners as she recognized the smell of roast chicken wafting up from the kitchen. "Well done, Rowan, thanks to your tirade you and your baby will eat well tonight."

Andrea couldn't help longing for just a taste herself but there was none on her tray when it came, just the same vegetable soup and two pieces of bread as always. Perhaps tomorrow they would cook up the bones and give her some. She took out the old clothes Mathew had given her and sat with them in her lap looking out at the moor, then she got her sewing kit and began to take in the waist of the trousers. They hadn't felt loose that first night, she mused as she pushed the needle through the heavy material, she must be losing weight. There, that would fit better.

Dusk was falling, might as well get ready.

Tingling with anticipation she straightened the high neck of the sweater under her chin and brushed her hair so it fell softly about her face, free of the sprays and lotions that usually controlled it. She watched the stars come out then eagerly awaited the man she no longer thought of as old.

Silently he led her through the fields and up the rough track. Although she breathed hard Andrea now felt no fear and when she looked about her she was surprised at how much she could see. Mathew had said her eyes would adjust.

As for him, he seldom spoke, except for the occasional muttered warning as they circumvented some bog or rough patch, or the valued word of praise when he found her still close behind him at the summit of a steep climb. It was enough, and she worked hard for these awards. When she stumbled, which was easy to do, she scrambled quickly to her feet hoping he hadn't noticed and she hardly felt any weariness as she sought to please him. When she returned home she was content to fall into her waiting bed and into a deep sleep, assured he would return again.

Getting Mathew to think well of her had become Andrea's goal. He was all she had, the only one in the whole world who cared, and during the day he remained on her mind as she relived each moment of their moorland rambles.

In this way her life developed a kind of order. Sleeping late, writing and sketching a little, and watching Rowan. She had become deeply concerned about the girl's welfare, each day carefully accessing her health and nearness to motherhood.

On this thirteenth drizzly cold morning of her imprisonment she fretted because the girl worked in the same clothes as always, the mist collecting in her hair, her face pinched and pale. As ever, though, the ribbon was fresh and new—the only thing that ever seemed to change. "Surely the child must be chilled to the bone," thought Andrea, who even behind her window was wearing a heavy turtleneck over another of her own. "Don't these people have jackets? She must be covered in goosebumps!" she worried aloud. "Let's see now, what have I...?"

She searched her belongings and pulled out a thick, woolen, zippered sweater. "Perfect!" She paused a moment. Was she talking out loud? "Well, what the hell, why not!" She resumed shaking out the garment and searching the pockets. This was the sweater Robert had once brought home from a trip to Canada. As she clutched it close she remembered him giving it to her. "Do you like it? The Cowichan Indians knit them." His eyes had sparkled but she had turned away.

"Thank you. You really shouldn't bother, you know. Dinner's ready, I have to be at a meeting by eight."

Why had she behaved that way? He always brought her things when he went away. Conscience gifts, she called them, for not having taken her. So many beautiful things... but would she have gone with him had he asked? Had he ever asked? She seemed to remember several times long ago... but surely he had never meant it... had he? Andrea stood, staring at nothing, then a cough brought her back to the present. Oh that poor kid, freezing down there.

She watched until the girl went into the tool shed, then bundled up the sweater and threw it as hard as she could so it landed not far from the bucket.

She just had time to duck back behind the curtain before Rowen returned carrying a trowel. At first the girl looked suspiciously at the alien lump. Then she tiptoed close, circled it once, picked it up then, between sending quick searching glances around her, inspected it. Now she held it against herself and finally, smiling broadly, she put it on and zipped it up to her chin. Big, bulky and comfortable she hugged herself in it, stroked it and straightened it, then skipped gleefully around the garden her cheeks as red as apples. Andrea clenched her hands together with delight. Then a shadow dulled her joy. Could she have made Rob feel this happy? Why had she never thanked him?

The girl was back at work, warm now and humming among the plants, pausing often to touch the wool and admire the thunderbird pattern.

Suddenly she stopped staking a tomato and looked toward the house. "Newt? Is that you?" she called.

"Aye, wot's up?" came his voice from indoors.

'It's wonderful. Fits a treat! Thank you, luv, thanks loads! Look, aren't I grand?" Rowan ran into the house.

Damn it! Andrea cowered against the wall. That brute was sure to know where the sweater came from. Would he tear it away from the girl and come raging upstairs after his prisoner? Andrea heard a footstep. No, no, it was nothing. Her face ached with the memory of his blow and she chewed her lip.

Look! There was Rowan running outside again still cozily enwrapped, a song bubbling from her lips. She ran over to the cat and picked it up, holding it near her face while she crooned, "Newt gave me a present. Newt gave me a present." Her hops and skips caused the cat to struggle free and flee for the bushes chased by happy laughter.

"That punk isn't so stupid—making himself look good," thought Andrea feeling a twinge of jealousy. Did Rowan have to be that grateful? To him who'd probably never done anything for anyone. After yesterday's fight too...

"Twas good of you to give that sweater to the lass," Mathew said when they'd passed through the gate that night.

"She looked cold," Andrea said, and as they walked on she was very glad her friend had guessed the truth.

It was a night darker than most with mist fraying edges and shortening distances. The fragrance of heather was strong and when Mathew left the trail, as he often did for short unexplained moments, Andrea broke off a twig and crumbling it between her fingers wandered contentedly on. The moors held no terrors now.

"Andy lass. I need help." The urgent call came from off to her left.

Andrea ran and found Mathew crouched over something. "What is it?"

"Ewe's snagged on bloody wire. 'Old her still now or 'twill pull tighter. Catch on 'ere. Mind, she's strong."

Andrea kneeled, hands buried deep in the wool of the ewe's neck, every muscle taut to stop the animal from struggling while Mathew fought to untangle the sharp barbs. She felt the warmth of the man beside her and heard his breath as he worked. Soon her arms ached until she thought she couldn't hold on another second but she gritted her teeth—choosing to go through agony rather than give in. Finally the sheep relaxed, the last tangle of wool released.

"Let 'er up."

The ewe scrambled to her feet and trotted off, stopping a short distance away to look back, lopsided from lying so long.

"What luck we found her!" Andrea exclaimed.

"Aye," Mathew said. "Already been there too long. Bloody shepherd should 'ave seen 'er. No dedication. Knew 'em all, we did. Checked 'em every day, oft times twice. Hush."

From far off there came excited bleating. Mathew gave a satisfied grunt and headed back toward the track.

Andrea still listened to the sound of the ewe rejoining her flock and as she did she thought of how Mathew always stopped to listen when they first left the garden, how he peered to left and right as they walked. She had assumed it was for their own safety but now she realized it was the sheep he was thinking of and keeping watch over. They were his purpose for coming out. It was they he listened for instead of talking.

She caught up and after a little while they passed through a dozing cluster of what looked like softly contoured boulders. Andrea stopped and looked at the slumbering sheep. They hadn't moved! She wanted to laugh aloud. For the first time the sheep paid no more attention to her than they did to Mathew!

She tugged at his sleeve. "They don't run!" she whispered. "They aren't afraid of me anymore!"

"Aye," he said. "They're used to you now."

"I'm so glad!" No one could know her happiness. She was accepted! She belonged! Her feet, light and sure on the turf, wanted to dance! And Mathew was smiling at her. He had never smiled before.

"Why do you care about them so much?" she asked.

"Been with 'em all my life one way or t'other."

"Then why don't you work still? I'd think you could use the money."

His back stiffened and he lengthened his stride so the gap between them widened.

Damn! She'd said the wrong thing. Why does he have to be so touchy? Just when things were going so well. And she had been so happy... Andrea, close to tears, stumbled and almost fell.

The figure ahead stopped to patch a hole in a wall and she wandered away and perched on a rock where the wind blew cold, lashing her hair against her cheeks. The fog had dissipated and there was only black sky above. It seemed to permeate her soul.

"Nay, Andy lass, I don't mean to be rough on ye." At first she thought his voice was the wind, then a hand gently rested on her shoulder. "You helped well back there." A short pause. "I like havin' your company."

Andrea didn't move. She just closed her eyes and all the blackness left. After a few moments she took the calloused hand in hers and turned it over. The palm was crisscrossed with streams of blood from the barbed wire he'd untangled from the sheep's fleece. Once there had been other hands with blood running across them. It was long ago when Leslie was still a baby. Robert had come indoors after pruning the pyracantha and Andrea had been on her way out to a meeting.

"Robert, you're bleeding..."

"You noticed..."

"Let me…"

"No, be on your way, I'm not helpless."

He'd headed toward the bathroom and she'd dashed off, smothering a knot of hurt beneath the day's plans.

Mathew's wire cut hands patiently waited.

"It's not only sheep that need looking after," she said huskily as she took out a kleenex and pressed it against the worst of the wounds. "We've got to get home and find some antiseptic."

"Aye, Lass, if you say so."

Was he laughing at her?

"Wait," Andrea whispered when they stood in the house's dark hallway. He nodded and she ran upstairs, snatched a bottle of peroxide from her make-up bag and rushed back down.

"Pour this over those cuts before they get infected," she ordered, then added, "You will, won't you?"

He took the bottle. "Aye, Andy Lass, I will. Thank you."

Something moved at the back of the house and Mathew slid away while Andrea fled upstairs not daring to breathe until she had closed her door behind her. She had taken for granted the fact that the punk went out at night, returning in the small hours of the morning and, trusting his absence, she had become less cautious. She could count on Rowan sleeping soundly. "But," she thought now, "What if that boy doesn't go out some night? If he caught us, it would be the end of everything." Newt was dangerous and unpredictable… and she must never forget it.

CHAPTER NINETEEN

The first thing Andrea did every morning when she awoke was to lie very still and listen for any hint that Rowen might be in trouble. Then, when that anxiety was assuaged, as it was now by the sound of humming that came from the garden, she let her mind drift back over the night before. She wondered how Mathew's hands were, and was suffused by a wave of tenderness as she remembered how trustingly he had held them out to her. Like Androcle's lion, she thought, smiling as she got out of bed and stretched, looking up at the ridgeline.

She dressed and tied her blue shirt at the waist admiring the fact that she actually had one again. Being hungry wasn't all bad, she mused as she walked to the bathroom, one actually got used to it, as one did to surviving with a modicum of washing. All those showers she used to take probably washed the oil out of her skin anyway. She hummed and was content with the face in the bathroom mirror. Whereas once she had looked for lines and aging now she only saw the brightness in her eyes and the alert, happy expression. "I used to check my dogs for that, " she said at the thought, then laughed aloud, a free happy sound.

Back at her room breakfast was steaming outside her door and the thought that Mathew had cared enough to time it so the porridge was hot filled her with gratitude.

She took the tray and sat comfortably in her chair near the window, relishing every spoonful from the heaping bowl as Rowan pottered below, snugly bundled in the Indian sweater. "I can't remember feeling so happy!" she mused as she set her spoon down. "How very odd! If it weren't for the punk this would truly be paradise." Yet in a way hadn't he made it all happen? Just a thug whose only interest in her seemed to be that she didn't escape and get him thrown out of his purloined home. At the moment she could almost thank him for it. Andrea thought back over the previous grey, passionless years. How wonderful it was to be alive again! Rowan to care for like a daughter and Mathew to love like... she stopped eating and rolled that last thought around her mind. Like what?

Sun warmed the air, the sweater was discarded and games with the cat interrupted weeding. The girl changed moods and occupations as quickly as cloud shadows flit across the garden.

"Are ye ready?" It was Newt calling from inside.

"Aye," she replied and undid her braid until her hair streamed long and gleaming across her shoulders.

Andrea leaned forward to better watch the boy who appeared carrying two buckets of water.

"Not too hot is it?" said the girl.

"Nay. Get yersel over here now. Look, I got the shampoo you like."

The buckets were set down and Rowan kneeled in front of one and dipped her head deep into the water.

The boy began to wash the sleek wet hair, massaging until shampoo foamed like a turban.

Rowan sat upright and swooped it into different shapes watching her shadow on the grass. "How do I look, Newt lad?"

"Like a queen. Smell like one too."

"Aye, I'm Queen of England I am. Come, my servant we mun hold court."

Rowan pranced up and down the little paths while the punk followed, bowing.

From Andrea's aerie they looked like two children playing and when their carefree laughter was joined by an extra loud chorus of birds, and two bees buzzed noisily around Andrea's window ledge, it felt as though the whole world was laughing.

Finally Newt rinsed the soap away finishing with the garden

hose while Rowan squealed at the coldness of it. With a worn towel they took turns rubbing the hair dry, then Rowan shook it loose in the sunlight, a waterfall of sunbeams.

"Where's my comb, Newt?"

"I'll get it." He disappeared and quickly returned.

Rowan took one look at the object he handed her and flung it into the row of cabbages. Instantly her face was transformed, crimson and strained, cords pushing her neck out of shape as she screeched, "Did you look at it? Did you? Half the teeth are broken! How can I use a comb like that? You fool! Let me go to the village and get a new one! You daft oaf!"

The cat disappeared in an orange streak. The birds went quiet. The bees zoomed away and even the breeze became still.

"I offered to buy you one..." The punk's words were drowned out by the enraged harangue that rose higher and higher as Rowan glared through her tangled mane.

"What a witch!" thought Andrea, then was shocked that she could think so of her beloved child.

"I'm going to t'village to buy meself a new comb." Defiantly Rowan marched toward the house only to be stopped short as Newt grabbed her arm and swung her roughly toward him.

"I know your plan. Trying to trick your way out of here. You mun stay put, Rowan, I'll not let you go."

"You used to let me out." She was whining now, an ugly sound.

"Just 'cause you stayed close by. Now you've got this bee in yer bonnet you're goin' no place. Not 'til after the baby's come."

Rowan burst into sobs and ran inside with the boy following.

"How strange?" murmured Andrea. "How very strange." The change had been so sudden and so absolute. She could hardly believe it had really happened.

A cloud covered the sun and foam from the tipped buckets soaked into the ground.

"Odd," she thought, shivering. "I almost felt sorry for that awful boy."

That night Andrea carried her boots downstairs and put them on out of earshot of the house, at the same time explaining to Mathew that they must be more careful in their comings and goings.

But he answered nothing and she knew his thoughts were already on the sheep. It bothered her that he seemed so unconcerned. Andrea sighed, she must keep alert for both of them.

The flock was peaceful so they climbed on for almost an hour until they reached a limestone outcropping. The wind was only a whisper as they rested against a large boulder with the moors stretched before them and a half moon above.

"Mathew?"

"Aye?"

"You once said you'd travelled. Where to?" She held her breath, wondering if this were safe territory, but hunger for conversation made her risk it.

"Eh, I've been all over. Australia, New Zealand, South America, Canada. Even near where you come from. It were a journey then. Not just a little plane trip. Life were very different. San Francisco's bridge was new. Reckon I'd know nowt about the place now."

"Tell me some of your adventures."

And he did. He who had previously seemed to ration each word now told the most wonderful stories, and she listened, fascinated, prodding him for more details and urging him back into his memories.

From that night on, after seeing that the sheep were safe, they would sit amid night sounds, sometimes looking out over starlit views, sometimes in the lee of a wall sheltered from wind or rain, and Mathew would talk, softly, as though to himself, going back in time. It was as though a dam had broken, letting stored words pour out in story after story and Andrea would lead him with the nudge of a question and a murmur of comprehension. His sharp wit made her laugh, and sometimes, as when he told of the death of a favorite dog, tears flowed as naturally as a summer shower.

She had never felt as comfortable with anyone... except maybe once long ago... and it felt natural to sit close for warmth and feel his sleeve brush her arm as they walked.

Weeks passed. Andrea was strong now and while they explored farther she learned about the countryside. Mathew explained how some of the walls had been built in the thirteenth century, few more recently than the end of the seventeenth. He pointed out how holes had been left for rabbits and other small creatures to pass from field to field, and showed where some waller had arranged a small hollow in stone so water could collect for the birds. He talked about sheep. Told with disgust how the breed had changed because all anyone was interested in was the meat so now the wool tended to be harsh and ugly. He described the birds and the countryside, and how things used to be, so she learned the Dales' history and saw them in sunlight even though it was always dark when she walked. She was amazed at his knowledge and came to believe he could answer any question she might ask—so long as it wasn't personal. If she did slip in that regard he might clam up for the rest of the night so she learned to be careful.

Above all she loved to watch him with the sheep, helping a new born twin get to its mother's milk where the stronger lamb already butted, or cleverly cornering a ewe to check out her lame foot. Always quiet, gentle and firm, she admired him immensely and loved when he asked her to help him. He taught her how to hold a ewe's head stable while he helped in a difficult birthing, or to recognize when one of the flock was missing and go after it, guessing where it might be.

Spring tiptoed into summer.

Andrea awoke from her afternoon nap feeling fingers of warm sunlight trailing across her. She had been here for over five weeks and no longer thought of herself as a prisoner. Thoughts of escape never crossed her mind, and she seldom thought of Robert's ashes. Looking after the sheep gave her life purpose, as did watching over the pregnant girl who was now very large. She had dared to mention, on one of their walks, that the baby needed to be well-nourished but Mathew had chuckled as he answered, "No need to worry about Rowan, she's eating well enough, Andy lass."

She loved being called that. Andy was the slimmed down woman who was eager to walk farther each night. Who chatted and laughed and cried with never a planned move. Who sometimes ran when the moon-washed track tempted, and who felt freer now than she had in her whole life.

It came as a shock when one night, as they sheltered under a tree to escape a heavy drizzle, Mathew asked about her life in America.

"Oh, no. I have nothing interesting to talk about. Not like you. I love your stories, Mathew. Please tell me more."

But he wasn't to be put off and continued to press her. "I want to hear about San Francisco, and you. Where did you live?"

Reluctantly she gave in and began, hesitantly at first, then the stories came. About those hikes in the East Bay parks when Leslie was a child, the time they'd seen the cougar, and when the three of them had been on a ferry crossing the bay and a whale had blown close enough to dampen them. She told about Robert becoming president of his company and taking her to dinner and dancing at the Top of the Mark to celebrate. The city below had been a fairyland of lights. Such wonderful stories...

And all lies...

"Why do I do it?" she asked Lesley's picture later. "Why do I lie to him of all people? He wouldn't care what I told him. He'd never judge me."

She thought over what she'd said. Sure, Robert had invited her out to celebrate his promotion but she'd refused, just as she'd been unable to go on those hikes with him and her son because of some business meeting she had to attend. She'd always been rushing in or out, had more important things to do than waste time... or be hurt.

Lesley's eyes looked sadly out at her and grief sat like lead in Andrea's chest. She longed to be with Mathew knowing his company would chase away her demons, but she must wait hours for that and, anyway, wasn't it he who had brought the whole thing up!

Last night's drizzle changed to steady rain. Rowan came out and wandered up and down the garden paths, seemingly oblivious to the downpour. At one time she sat on the grass and picked daisies which she wove into a chain and draped around her neck, then she returned calls to a cuckoo until Andrea couldn't tell which was the real bird. The sweater's sleeves drooped from heaviness and straightened curls sent rivulets into the girl's eyes, but she appeared not to notice.

Andrea grew frantic and it was all she could do to stop from calling out. For once she longed to hear the punk ordering Rowan indoors. Telling her she'd catch pneumonia.

Oh foolish child can't you feel the rain!

"Coom, lass." At last! Newt strode to Rowan, took her hand and pulled her inside.

Andrea relaxed and began to write in the diary which had begun as Robert's letter. For a while she worked, then broke off to put the end of the pen in her mouth and stare at nothing. Something about that earlier scene in the garden kept intruding, nagging at her so she couldn't concentrate. Something was wrong but she didn't know what. Perhaps Rowan was just reacting to the moods of pregnancy.

That night when she was handed her usual fare of soup, bread and tea she whispered, "You will take me out tonight, won't you?"

"In this?" They could both hear the rain drumming on the slate roof. "Nay, Lass, you'd catch your death."

Usually in really bad weather Mathew didn't come for her

and she didn't expect him to, but Andrea knew he went to the moor anyway—no hurting creature would be made to suffer through a night just because of rain. But tonight she needed him as much as any of them. Only his solid, loving presence could help calm the intangible whisps of memory that had swirled like midges about her since their talk last night—and her confusion about Rowan.

"Please. I don't mind getting wet," she begged. "Please?"

For a moment he was quiet, then he nodded.

The heavy drops that beat on her head felt good. The sheep were crowded snugly in a sheltered corner and when Mathew turned back toward home she pleaded that instead he take her up onto the moor. He seemed reluctant, then reading the need in her, wordlessly led the way.

Andrea reveled in the lashing of the storm as she leaned into the wind. A harder curtain of rain raced over them until the deluge was like drowning and Mathew tugged her into the lee of a wall where the downpour missed them, slicing overhead in a wind driven frenzy. They crouched, huddled side by side, gaining warmth from each other—like a couple of sheep.

It was a private, safe world with just her and this gentle man. Outside the rain drummed and the wind howled. Andrea watched a droplet run down a stalk of grass. Watched a small bush bend almost horizontal, and wondered at how strong its roots must be to not let it be torn up and whisked away. She could feel her own roots wanting to do the same. To cling and stay here, safe and undisturbed forever.

"Why did it upset you to talk about your home?"

As it often did, Mathew's voice seemed more like one of her own thoughts, but this time it seemed to stir a deviant chill, that brought visions of her house and son, Rob and herself, all as ugly comic strip characters in an ugly comic strip life. "Upset? What do you mean?" she said. But he knows, she thought, he recognizes pain, but I don't have to admit it. Not yet anyway. Not quite yet. I don't know what to say. I don't understand it myself. "I'd just rather listen to you," she said." You haven't told me about Starwell. What kind of people live there?"

She felt him looking at her.

"Tell me," she insisted. "Please, I want to know."

He put his arm around her, and her cheek rested on his shoulder. "Can't say as I know much about them as live 'ere now. A lot of city folk are buying from t'owd uns. Tearing down and building finer places. When I were a lad though, the place were bustling. Aye, we all knew everyone and every animal abaht t'place."

"How old were you when you first came?"

"Eh, I were born nearby. In a farmhouse near the 'ead of the beck that runs down through the village. My father were well off for 'ere abouts. That's 'cause he handled 'is sheep right. Made us lads work 'ard but made us go to school too which a lot o' dads didn't—and church."

The words fell softly, flickering like a fire, warming their space, making Andrea safe again.

He was silent for a moment, remembering, then he continued and as the rain pounded around them Andrea delighted in old Percy, the rag and bone man; Thomas the postman who pushed his bicycle up to their lone house whatever the weather, to be welcomed with lemonade in summer and hot chocolate in winter, and a lot of the other characters who had inhabited Mathew's boyhood.

"Then mother died, alone in the house, while the rest of us searched for sheep buried in the previous night's blizzard."

His sadness turned the falling rain to tears and Andrea knew that the one word "alone" had weighed heavily on him for years. Her hand crept out and took his.

"She'd been poorly for some time, though she'd made light of it and kept up with her work. Even smiling became an effort. I could see that, but kids don't want to believe there's anything wrong with them as they love. She even wanted to come out with us that day, but dad persuaded her to stay by t'fire. 'Er spirit just slipped away while she sat there. When we came back the house was still warm and she welcomed us with a smile that had never left."

"How old were you?"

"Ten. She were a fine woman. A dreamer, even though 'er life were all work. "Mathew," she'd say, "Don't ever forget to notice the rainbows, too many folk see only the rain.""

For a while they sat in silence while Andrea wondered how different she would have been if she'd followed that maxim.

"Your dad. What happened to him?"

"He were never the same after she went. The 'eart were fair gone out of 'im. I reckon he never told her how he felt about her though, it's hard for a Yorkshireman. A body needs to know they're cared about or they grow a shell outside and scar from the loneliness inside."

"I care for you, Mathew."

"I know, lass. I know." He turned and his kiss was so gentle it was as though he touched her soul.

Andrea shivered.

"Coom, Lass, we mun be off. Look, the rain's lightened."

Indeed, it was the noise of a nearby streamlet that was loudest now and droplets loitered on grass tips until the wind shook them free. Mathew stood up, leaving a chill beside her, then reached down and pulled her to her feet, so they stood looking into each other's eyes, then they both smiled, and started hand in hand for home down the rain puddled trail.

Inside the house she looked back from half way up the stairs. He was soaking wet and she loved him so. She waved farewell.

"I'm amazingly happy!" Andrea said to her bedraggled reflection in the mirror. "He loves me!" she whispered to the girl in the photo. "Just me!" Scarcely aware of how wet and cold she was she peeled off her garments, dried herself, put on her pajamas and jumped into bed, curling into a tight ball for warmth. Soon she was comfortable but her mind stayed busy hearing Mathew's voice, remembering what he'd said about his childhood. Suddenly she sat up and snapped on the light. Above her on the wall was the needlepoint and she read again, 'Mathew and his Dog.' That boy was her Mathew! She pictured his gentle, hard working mother sitting up some cold night long ago, sewing with loving, weary fingers.

Within seconds she was asleep, dreaming she was on the moor running with a young, dark haired man. When they reached a huge limestone outcropping he turned and caught her in his arms, hugging her so she could scarcely breathe. She looked into the well of his eyes and her soul trembled with joy. She loved the smell of him. The smell of heather and sheep...

But it wasn't Mathew, she realized in a moment of wakefulness, the man in her dream was Robert.

Next morning something stopped her from opening the door when she heard the usual tap announcing breakfast. Instead she waited until the footsteps had gone, then retrieved the tray left outside. It was the same at suppertime, she waited until the bearer had retreated before collecting her meal. But in the dark later she was ready for her Mathew to take her to the moors.

There was an easiness between them now and they needed no words as she helped him listen for trouble among the sheep, circled away from him to look at a small group distanced from the rest, waited, ready to help when he did the same. She felt joy that he trusted her and they shared delight when they found the ewe expected to lamb a week before now had twins curled next to her. Andrea rejoiced in her ability to see in the dark, the increasing lightness of her step, the thrill of running to her friend with some news, or something she'd found, knowing he'd be interested. And she loved the way he stroked her face, and played with her hair when they talked. She wanted more. Wanted him to make love to her, but something warned her that could not be.

"Show me where you lived with your parents," she asked one night, and immediately wished she hadn't. He seemed turned to stone, to even stop breathing.

"It sounded so beautiful," she encouraged.

Still he stood silent and Andrea, trying to rectify some terrible gaffe, said quickly, "Never mind, we can walk along the tops."

"No, it's time I went." Mathew was already striding off to the right and she ran to catch up.

He seemed to have forgotten her as they climbed higher than ever before in a southerly direction. The wind picked up, pushing them on and Andrea played with the idea that it might tear the darkness away and leave them stranded in daylight. Soon a more likely worry arose that they were going too far and would never get back before Newt but she daren't say anything. Mathew was like a machine which couldn't stop until it arrived at its destination.

They traversed a bog on a narrow spongy trail Andrea couldn't even see, crossed a ridge and finally dropped down to where a gate blocked their way. Mathew leaned his forearms on the top rail and stared into a shallow valley, little more than a fold in the hills. It was an isolated place with no hint of light or habitation. His breath shuddered in his throat. "That were my father's farm," he said.

Andrea looked down into a darkness full of things only he could see. "Where's the house?" she whispered.

Mathew pointed toward a darker patch—probably a grove of trees.

Andrea could just make out a solider smudge off to one side and imagination made it the corner of a building. "Does someone live there now?"

"Aye." It sounded like a snarl. "Some big city lawyer type. Stole it from me while I were gone, they did. My brothers were all too happy to take the brass and sit in front of TVs in town. Didn't wait for my say… and all the time I were away I dreamed of coming back and running my own flock. I'd finally made enough to buy it off of 'em." His tone, so bitter, changed to a deep sadness. "I loved the place."

Andrea felt a jungle of things unsaid. Was it something to do with this that caused him to live like an outcast, out only by night? You don't have to tell me until you want to, she thought, and moved closer hoping he felt her sympathy.

After a while they silently walked back home.

They returned the next night and leaned again on the still sun-warm gate to look down into that private, hidden world from Mathew's past. After that it seemed a compulsion for him to return night after night. He spoke freely of his time there and Andrea could almost hear the sound of children's voices and the clip clop of pony feet. It was as though he wanted to bring back a time when life was good and eliminate whatever came after. She wondered what that was.

"What would you do if it were yours now?" She asked.

"I'd be at work on a shed to shelter the sheep next winter. Buy the best ram I could find and some good ewes. And I'd get me a fine pup to train... but it's all dreams."

"Couldn't dreams be some of the rainbows your mother talked about?"

Mathew was quiet a moment. "Eh, Andy, nobbut you're right. And I guess there's not much but dreams for you and me, is there?"

"Can't they be enough?" she said, softly. "Tell me again what the house is like inside."

Mathew looked up at the stars.

How beautiful he is, like a Michelangelo sculpture, Andrea thought. If I touched his face would it be cold like marble? She had once seen blind children running their hands over a statue in a museum and envied them the intimate knowledge they attained through their fingertips. How she longed to reach out now...

"We'd have to modernize the kitchen."

We. She trembled with joy. He included me! We'll do it together. Dream together.

"Put in a good heating system. Mum was allus so bitter cold away from the fire."

Andrea wanted to ask if his mother did petit point there, but then she would have to tell him about the piece she'd found, and feel obligated to offer it to him. Instead she said, "We'd not want to make it look too modern." And to herself she thought, 'And, dear Mathew, we'll keep each other warm.'

"I think I might knock out a wall to make the parlor bigger. Put in a big window."

"How many rooms are there?"

Mathew counted, leading Andrea through each one as they decorated and planned.

"It's a wonderful house!" she enthused.

"Aye, it is, isn't it!" He laughed, a wonderful sound she'd never heard before.

"I love you," she whispered.

He put his fingers across her lips. "Eh, Lass," he murmured in a way that made her want to cry.

In the nights that followed that spot became their place to enter another world. A world that gave each what they most wanted, and in Andrea's mind the valley was as much hers as Mathew's.

CHAPTER TWENTY

The bigger and more awkward Rowan grew the more she fought with Newt, and each battle fueled Andrea's loathing for the punk who held them captive, although now she herself had no wish to leave.

Only the calico cat seemed free to come and go as it pleased. Andrea would watch it prowling through the garden or lying in the sun outside the kitchen, and then one afternoon, to her delight, a small mew at her door announced that he had found her and she let him in. The tigerish creature wound around the room exploring, rubbed once against Andrea's legs then slid back out. But the next day he came again and soon Andrea took to leaving the door ajar so he could come and go as he pleased. She named him Tigger, and when he was in an especially affectionate mood he would sit on her lap and purr while she stroked the raggedy orange coat.

Having the door open also made it easier to listen to the music Newt played on his guitar each morning. First there was Rock, loud and raucous, exactly what one would expect from its punk creator, but after a while the music would change, starting and stopping, altering to a more gentle mood. Composing. For a long time Andrea wouldn't admit that that awful youth could create something beautiful, but finally she had to, and often a tune would stay in her mind and she'd find herself humming it later in the day.

He put words to his music too, although she could seldom make them out... until he wrote the lullaby for Rowan. Andrea listened to him slowly putting it together, a wistful, sweet tune, to which he lastly added lyrics. Silence. The music began again with something else. Andrea crept onto the landing to hear better and realized it was Rowan singing along in her whispery voice. It was beautiful and sad.

She heard that song often after that. When Newt joined Rowan in the garden they would wander the paths of their green, flowered wilderness singing it together. Andrea knew the words now. "Little baby, Rowan's own, the world waits for you to come. Happiness will live with you, For Rowan loves her baby true." Simple words. Rabbits scampered from patch to patch while Tigger lay in his favorite clump of forget-me-nots and blinked. The pregnant girl would for a time be tranquil and the garden world was serene.

CHAPTER TWENTY-ONE

The moors changed where wildflowers grew among the bent. Sometimes Andrea longed to be out in daylight, walking in color instead of grey and white, but the night was friendly and belonged to her and Mathew. She dug out her sewing kit and took her trousers in another inch, then she went through the rest of her clothes. Many of the styles and colors offended her. They suited some other woman in some other place and she put them away. She felt most comfortable in the old jacket and pants Mathew had given her. How long ago was that? Two months? She'd lost count.

The woman in the mirror was always a surprise and Andrea enjoyed each meeting. The cheeks were flushed and the eyes sparkled. Her hair, almost back to its natural brown tumbled to her shoulders and she had to keep pushing back the one strand that insisted on falling forward. She did so now, and smiling, said aloud, "I'm not so old!"

A rush of warmth went out to this familiar self who had returned from the past, yet somehow she had the strange feeling she'd looked at it every day.

Anticipation of escaping to the moor with Mathew was never far away. She was constantly thinking of things to tell him: A thought, a dream, a question about an unfamiliar bird she'd heard that afternoon, an idea for the house. And he never let her down, whatever the weather, no matter how late, as was infrequently caused by a visit from Newt's friends, he would come for her.

Sometimes when they were together she thrilled to the knowledge he needed her too and knew from the freedom of his laugh that she was good for him and had given him new life as he had her.

Then without warning, when everything seemed perfect, fear tangled around her heart, warning that such joy could only be transitory, and she clung to the moment, panicked, afraid to let it slip away in case there was more of that good time behind her than there was to come.

That cloud passed and happiness again prevailed.

Sometimes she ran along the trails she now knew so well. Once when Mathew caught up to her standing on a bluff waiting for him he laughed. "Andy lass, are you the same as said she couldn't walk the home field a short while back?"

"I feel so strong, Mathew. I can't believe it!" She took his hand and pulled him along to walk beside her. "Once I saw a piece of sculpture in an art gallery in Tiburon. Done in Lucite by an artist named Hart, I remember. The outer form was a face but when you looked past that, inside glowed a complete woman, pure, ethereal, yet very alive! That inner being entranced me. I've always remembered it. Now I recognize it as me. The inner me. You and the moor found me again. Set me free." She stopped. "I sound crazy."

Mathew turned to face her, took both her hands, and smiled. "I allus did see the glow of you, Andy lass, it just needed a little dreampolish."

"Aye, mebbe that's it."

His smile broadened. "And we've got you speaking a bit of Yorkshire too!"

She laughed and together they ran to the gate overlooking Mathew's valley and leaned on it, shoulder to shoulder, in a wonderful feeling of oneness. They discussed buying a couple of horses and whether an elder bush planted by the door would really keep flies away.

Then one night Mathew took off toward the left after they'd checked the sheep.

Andrea stopped short. "Where are we going?"

"Thought you might like to see the village."

Don't go, something inside her warned. Don't go. "Can we? I mean is it safe?" Curiosity cancelled further argument.

"Aye, no one'll see us and the lad's away at a gig in Otley."

They had reached a well travelled path across a meadow and before them the river ran, wide and quiet. Andrea caught up and walked beside him. They crossed a footbridge, stopping to look down at the sleek, dark water that murmured over and around the lighter shapes of rocks. Then the trail took them into the secretive shadow of trees and Andrea felt nervous away from the familiar moor. They ducked under a low branch.

"What kind of a gig?" she asked needing the assurance of Mathew's voice.

"A Rock festival. His group were asked. Newt were right thrilled about it."

"You mean he's a professional musician?" She'd never thought of him being anything but her jailer.

"Aye. He's right champion too!"

Andrea was surprised at the pride in Mathew's voice. "He gets paid?"

"Aye. How do you think he puts food on our table? It's hard though for a lad to keep four folk on what he gets at local gigs. He'd go far if it weren't for us. He's a rare talent is Newt."

Andrea imagined that wildly painted creature in front of an audience, being applauded, perhaps adored by teenagers, and no one would have any idea … "Then why on earth…?"

"Shh, 'ere's the road. Best be quiet now." He helped her over the last stile and their feet hit tarmac.

It was exciting to walk along the street, cottages all dark. At one a dog barked but no lights came on. The smell of ale hung around the pub and for a moment Andrea stopped to look longingly through a small shop's window at some dates. She used to love dates.

"This way," Mathew whispered, and pushed through a small gate. Andrea followed and realized the path led up to a church. She stopped.

"You asked about t'place once. Like you had a special interest or summat." He guided her around the side of the stone building to where rows of gravestones gleamed dully as far as the night allowed her to see.

Andrea couldn't breathe. Although she wanted to run the other way something drew her forward, alone, across the grass to a corner under a giant yew where a small stone stood half covered by weeds. She kneeled and pushed back the growth, trying to read the inscription. If only there were a moon... but finally she found an angle and managed to decipher the words: "Lesley Clayton. She chose her time." She read it again, and the dates of her birth and death. Whatever did it mean... "She chose her time?" Such a cold epigraph. Almost an indictment. Andrea sat back on her heels. She had expected something larger. More elaborate. This grave only looked small and neglected. A wave of pity suffused her. Poor Lesley. So young. "I loved you once," thought Andrea wistfully. "Wanted so much to be like you." Then the face in the portrait floated in front of her. "You haven't brought the ashes," it accused.

"Damn you!" Andrea sprang to her feet. "Damn you!" She rushed back to the gate and leaned against it trembling.

Mathew coughed. She had forgotten him standing in the shadows, and for the first time wondered if he'd met Lesley. How much did he know?

He shifted his cap and joined her.

"Mathew, did..." But her question was never asked because at that moment a car came around the bend, shining bright headlights on the place where she would have been had Mathew not yanked her out of view.

"Best not let anyone see us," he said.

Andrea stayed leaning against him, trying to shake the confusion left by Lesley's grave.

"We mun get back," he said gently.

They walked in silence, each deep in thought, returning up the road, across the bridge and through the gate Andrea had struggled with on that rainy afternoon on what seemed a lifetime ago. She felt an enormous sense of relief when they reentered their own garden, and inside the house she clung to Mathew's hand loath to let go—wanting to pour out all her uncertainties and premonitions—but not understanding them enough to put into words.

Why hadn't they just roamed the moor as usual?

"It's all right," he whispered as though reading her mind, and she left him.

As she waved from the top of the stairs she told herself that nothing was different, but when she got into bed she curled up, pressing into the mattress as though to fuse herself to the present. "Don't make me leave," she pleaded. "Please don't let it end."

She couldn't sleep until the first rustlings of the first birds, and then she had nightmares she couldn't remember past waking.

Peace was gone. Even Rowan frittered disconsolately in the garden, and downstairs Newt played the loud, discordant music that only irritated. Andrea longed for night and every moment that separated her from Mathew seemed an eternity.

Toward evening a storm threatened.

This night was blacker than any Andrea had known and she stayed close to Mathew lest she lose him. They moved slowly because of the wind that tried to hurl them backward and when they reached the sheep it was difficult to be certain they were all there. Finally they both agreed that the lamb with the one black foot was missing. They counted again to make sure, then separated to search. Deafened by the wind Andrea stumbled blindly about growing ever more desperate as she thought of the little thing lost and alone on a night like this. She almost fell into the beck that raced and leapt down the hill. Surely it wouldn't have tried to cross... then she saw the white, sodden rag at the edge of the water. She crouched to make sure. Its tiny dark nose swayed with the current, its hind legs still on land, the wind catching its tail so it almost looked alive. Andrea stared, tears hot on her face in contrast to the cold rain that had begun to strike her. Suddenly she was pushed aside. "It's alive!" said Mathew, lifting the lamb back onto land and frantically massaging its ribs until it snorted several times, then uttered a series of hoarse little coughs.

Andrea watched, witnessing a miracle.

"Ere, you hug 'im warm. We'll take 'im back to the house. Needs warming through he does."

He helped her put the sodden little creature inside her heavy sweater and though it felt cold against her chest she filled with delight to feel his shivering life against her.

"Coom Lass, we mun get you back afore ye both catch yer deaths."

They faced into the storm for a way then headed downward with it trying to knock their feet sideways from under them. It seemed forever until Andrea saw the wind-tossed shapes of familiar trees and, with a shudder of relief, recognized the row of shrubs by the back gate. The house had never been so welcome.

But Mathew had stopped at the iron wicket.

Andrea tried to push around him. 'What's the matter?' Then she saw and recoiled in horror. What she had feared and dreaded most had happened, the punk had come home early and discovered her absence. Every light in the house was on, catching on the raindrops and reaching like a net to capture her.

CHAPTER TWENTY-TWO

"What'll we do!" She grasped for Mathew but he broke away and loped toward the door. "Mathew!" Her wail was lost in rain that pounded harder by the second. She leaned against the gatepost clutching the lamb and shivering, wondering what to do, her brain numb. At any moment that punk would emerge, raging out after her. There he was now, silhouetted, but no it was Mathew.

"Andy! Andy! Coom!" He called, hands cupped to his mouth.

Wind snicked the gate shut behind her and Andrea's thoughts raced as she automatically responded to the familiar call for help. What could need assistance here? The answer came like a flash of lightening. The girl.

Rowan! Andrea thrust herself away from the post and ran as fast as she could up the path, arms aching from steadying her burden, puddles splashing, roar of rain in her ears. She ran straight to Mathew who took the lamb from her, then on into the kitchen and to the bed in the corner. Huddled in the middle of it was Rowan who just at that moment let out a scream that quickly distracted Andrea from the shock of seeing Newt in full make-up, mohawk stiff as wire, bent over, awkwardly wiping the girl's face with a damp cloth. "Are ye all right?" he kept asking in a voice panicky and young. Relief lit his heavily lined eyes at sight of Andrea. "Help 'er," he croaked, taking a step backward.

"What's happening?" Rowan's question ended in a whimper then her eyes focused on Andrea. "Who are you? Mother? Oh

Newt, it's killing me!"

"Hush, 'ush, you'll be fine," he said. "She's t' lady from upstairs, remember? She'll 'elp you 'ave yer baby."

She doesn't even know me, thought Andrea. How can that be when I know her so well? "Get me some towels and something to wrap the child in when it arrives," she ordered the punk.

Rowan moaned and gripped Andrea's hand until the bones felt ready to crumble but she savored the pain and the chance to finally be with and help the girl she had watched for so long. "It's all right," she soothed, praying it was. After all what did she know about birthing babies? She and Rob had gone to classes. He had been so kind and patient, rushing home from work, missing supper. She hadn't thought about it at the time. "Breathe deep, slow." She could hear him saying it as she did now for this fragile, frightened creature, face flushed and hair tangled over the pillow.

She should be in hospital. What if something went wrong? Why wasn't there a phone in this damn place! Andrea ran her free hand through her hair to squeeze out the rainwater, and dabbed her face with the corner of a blanket.

Rowan screamed.

"For a Chris' sake go get a doctor!" Andrea shouted at the boy who hovered by the stove.

"No!" The voice came from next to her ear. Rowan's eyes blazed as she half reared up. "No doctor!" Breathing pain she sank back and began to give high little wails like a child's, that got increasingly louder until Andrea wanted to scream too.

Newt ran over. "It's all right, Rowan, there'll be no doctor." He stroked the golden hair and as Rowan's eyes fixed on his her wailing stopped. "No doctor," Newt repeated gently." Don't ever say otherwise," he warned Andrea. "There'll be no mention o' doctors in this 'ouse. She's 'ad 'er fill o' them." He never took his painted, worried eyes off the girl who lay looking up at him as a child would at its parent.

"Can I have a ribbon? A cherry red one?" she whispered.

"Aye, I'll get you a cherry red one."

"Let's sing, Davey."

He began the lullaby, very softly, and she joined in.

"Little baby, Rowan's son…"

Andrea had been watching with an increasing feeling of strangeness and from her memory came the voice of a young man in a pub long ago saying he'd been in Starwell on business looking for someone. Hadn't the woman in the purple hat said he worked in a mental hospital? Suddenly in a flash of understanding all the odd incidents in the garden fell into place. "Why she's…"

'She's not crazy," snapped the boy. "Just can't grow up is all."

Why had she never seen it? The quick changes of mood… childishness had seemed so natural in the garden. An enormous sadness arose in Andrea, and a feeling of loss—her perfect child… the magic had not been real.

Fingers tightened on her hand, bringing her back—she must deal with that later—now Rowan had her baby to deliver. The contractions were very close.

"It's okay. You're doing fine," she whispered.

Was she? Andrea fought to still her own panic. Just because she'd had a baby didn't mean she knew anything. Wheeled into an operating room, anesthetized. In newspapers women had babies in taxis with the help of the cab driver, by the side of the freeway assisted by a kindly police officer. One woman, she remembered, was even helped by her six year old daughter. How had they all known what to do? In movies people were always advising the mothers to push or not to push. Appalled by her ignorance Andrea did, however, remember the pain of labor and how it helped to have someone to hold on to. She recalled the strength she'd received from her husband's long strong hand and how soothing his voice had been. He'd been there all that time. His eyes so kind, so worried. Dear Robert!

"Why do I hurt so?"

Andrea could feel the pain herself as the young woman cried

out, and she murmured under her breath, "Robert, Robert. Oh Robert where are you now!" But he wasn't here. "I can't do this!" Andrea, panicked, loosened her hand and stepped away, but as she did her eyes were drawn toward a dark corner of the room where another pair of eyes met and held her gaze. They told her to remember the lambings on the moor and how capable she had been. Reassured her that she wasn't alone. "Mathew." All the panic left her in the sigh that was his name and she was strong again.

"When did the pains begin?" she asked the girl.

"Bout noonish. Didn't say owt though. Mustn't upset Newt. Wouldn't have gone to work. 'E trusts me to stay alone, y'know. Sez he's proud o' me. Owoo!"

"Lucky I came home early." Sweat glistened through the punk's white makeup and Andrea realized with satisfaction that he was more terrified than she was.

The baby should come soon. Andrea went to the sink and washed her hands. She was calm now. Newt was forgotten. There was only Rowan, the struggling infant and herself.

Time passed, then suddenly it was over. A small wet creature slid onto the bed and Rowan lay quietly panting as though at the finish of a race. Andrea looked at the tiny being, lost as to what to do next. But Mathew was there picking the slippery newborn up as he had done many a lamb, making sure it could breathe, then laying it gently on Rowan's belly. "String," he said, and a moment later Newt handed over Rowan's yellow hair ribbon which Mathew carefully tied around the umbilical cord. "Summat to cut with."

Andrea held her hand out toward Newt and after a moment felt something slapped against her palm. A knife. The knife he had threatened her with. Laughter bubbled inside her as she passed it to Mathew. The baby whimpered. Could such a small thing live? It wailed. Newt produced a blanket which Andrea wrapped around it, then the three of them crowded close, entranced by such miniature perfection. Only the mother did not share their excitement. She lay with her face to the wall.

"You take it." Newt picked up the bundle and held it toward her. "Rowan it's yer lad. 'E's a beaut." The punk's voice pleaded.

Andrea looked at the still figure in the bed and knew it was not sleeping. Knew its every nerve was stiffened against the presence of this child, and suddenly she was cold, wet and furious. She leaned over and grabbed Rowan's shoulders. "Damn it, Rowan, take your baby!"

The girl turned like a cornered cat.

"You take it, and hug it and feed it." Andrea forced the child into reluctant arms. Arms more robot than mother.

"Wot d'you want to name him?" Newt asked.

"What do you want to name him?" Once, long ago, Robert had stood over her bed, his face soft for her and their son.

She had loved him so much at that moment. Wanted to give him the world. "Leslie Clayton James. We'll call him Leslie, with an 'ie'. You'd like that wouldn't you, Darling?"

He'd looked surprised and had tried to argue her out of it, but she'd insisted, knowing what pleasure it must really give him. Finally he'd given in.

"Makes no difference to me," Rowan mumbled.

"Well, wot about Sting! 'Ow about that? D'ye like it?" The punk's tone placated the mother as he tried to make the child human and not the uninvited insect Rowan's expression insinuated. "'Ow about that, little Sting, eh?" He touched the child's fingers very, very gently.

Andrea glanced toward Mathew who had moved back into the shadows and she was shaken to see stark fear in his eyes as he stared not at the baby but at its mother. "Something's going on here I don't understand," Andrea thought. "Nobody's acting the way they should." She felt let down and depressed. She had worried about this baby for so long, and loved its mother.

A strand of wet hair fell across her face and as she pushed it back she became aware of her sodden clothes and muddy boots.

Good Lord! Surely the punk must have noticed. Had he checked her room? Maybe he'd just gotten home. Perhaps he'd been too preoccupied to think about where she'd come from or what she looked like. Oh pray God it was true. But it couldn't last. At this moment he seemed completely absorbed in the mother and child—but soon he must notice her condition. Perhaps if she crept away now…

Upstairs Andrea peeled off her unbearably clammy clothes and it wasn't until she'd toweled herself and put on her warmest pajamas that she could think of anything else. Then she began to worry about that poor tiny soul whose mother didn't seem to want it. "I should be downstairs helping… I should never have left," she thought. Was that a baby's cry? It was hard to tell with the rain still pounding down. Did he even have a bed? Andrea hurried across the room and looked outside at the reflection from the kitchen lights. What was going on? And what about the lamb? Where was it? For a moment she felt good thinking about that. Mathew would see that it was warm and cozy somewhere. Her door squeaked and opened slightly to let the calico cat slide through. It stopped, white tipped paw raised, and yellow staring eyes on hers.

"What's the matter, Tigger? Has the baby upset you?"

With a bound it came to her and began rubbing its thin, damp, orange and black body around her legs, and when she sat down it immediately sprang onto her lap and began to purr. Andrea's hand automatically stroked while her ears strained for any sound. Finally she could bear it no longer and nervously stood up, spilling the annoyed cat to the floor. They both went into the hall where Andrea leaned over the banister while the cat padded silently down. It was deathly quiet. Were they all asleep?

Andrea yawned and went to bed, pulling the blankets up and wrapping them around her like a cocoon. Thunder rumbled. As she became warmer she dreamily reminisced about her own baby and how for a short time she and Robert had worked together looking after him, keeping him warm, fed and loved.

As she drifted toward sleep she continued to follow Leslie through his infancy, Robert by her side. She even heard him whispering one day into that tiny ear, "Leslie, you're perfect. Just like your mother."

But that wasn't the way it was! Andrea sat bolt upright, staring into the darkness and the past. He had said like "her". Hadn't he? And of course he'd meant Leslie's namesake… but which had it really been? Wind rattled the window as though someone were trying to get in.

Andrea struggled to remember the truth of what had happened that day so long ago. She had heard—or thought she heard—that hateful comparison—and stopped unseen in the doorway. Heart filled with bitterness she'd turned away and that very afternoon found an au pair who cared for the baby until he was able to go to nursery school. She and Robert were seldom alone together with him after that.

Andrea stared into the darkness. The storm quieted. She closed her eyes and saw her baby's face. The square chin, the swirling dark hair, the little ears with lobes larger than most. Lobes like hers.

Andrea's fists clenched and she drew a deep shuddering breath.

Outside an owl moaned. Little Sting! Was he warm down there? Did they have diapers? She hadn't seen any. Had Rowan fed him? Quickly Andrea slipped into her bathrobe and crept down and along the empty hallway to the open kitchen door. The room beyond was dark and warm. She listened for a second then stepped carefully toward Rowan's bed wondering if the baby would be there or in a crib of some sort. A faint sound caused her to step back against the wall and freeze. Someone else was awake in the room. What were they doing? Moving so stealthily. There was a sound like a small sneeze. Then silence.

Andrea's skin crawled and the hair on her neck rose. For a while she waited then she fled back up to her bed where she lay under the covers trembling.

It was daylight when she awoke but her mind was still with

the night before. She could hear nothing from downstairs and, with a rapidly beating heart, hurried down. Gentle snores came from the pantry but nothing moved in the kitchen corner where Rowan lay. First Andrea stopped by the oven. The door was partially open and the heat on low. Inside she could just make out a box in which curled the lamb. She put her hand in to touch the warm body, and felt the even patter of its heart. It curled tighter. Andrea smiled, stroked it gently. then moved away.

She tiptoed toward Rowan who lay on her side, hair covering her face. She seemed fast asleep, but then Andrea caught a gleam amongst the strands and knew the girl watched her.

A small, homemade cradle yawned empty blankets beside the bed.

"Peek-a-boo, I see you." Rowan's voice was a singing whisper.

"Do you have the baby, Rowan? Is he there?"

"Do you want to see him? Shall I let you? Does he want to see you? He's mine you know, a man gave him to me. I tried to give him back, someone told me who to see, but nasty Newt wouldn't let me go."

Is that what the fights in the garden had been about? Not escape at all, but abortion? "Where is he Rowan?"

The new mother looked down toward her breast under the covers. "Little Sting. So cold. Hug, hug you warm."

"Let me see him, Rowan. Please."

"Promise not to take him. Newt says he's mine forever."

"I promise."

For a moment the bright eyes studied her then suddenly the girl turned onto her back and held the child aloft. It was naked but for the yellow ribbon tied too tightly around its neck. And it didn't move.

CHAPTER TWENTY-THREE

"Isn't he beautiful? He's all mine. A ribbon for each day like me, but he has no hair. Newt said he'd get me a cherry red one today." Then she sang in her little whispery voice, "Rowan lass has a lad, he will make her very glad." She whisked the child under the covers. "Cold, cold, cold."

"Please may I touch him?"

Again the calculating stare. "Okay. Can't hold him though."

Andrea reached forward and took the little hand that flopped from the covers, then moved her own hand upward until she could feel his cheek. All so cold and dead. "Oh Rowan!" Her heart was ready to break.

But Rowan smiled up with childish happiness. "Isn't he beautiful?"

Andrea straightened, finding it hard to breath. "Yes, Rowan dear, he's very beautiful." She looked toward the far door behind which the men must be sleeping. Let them cope with it, there was nothing she could do now.

She fled, stumbling upstairs toward her sanctuary where she sat in her chair, hugging her robe about her, looking out toward the awakening moor and the tail of departing black clouds. She tried not to think of what she'd seen but below the garden seemed to tremble with the ghost of a fey, happy girl and the promise of new life. A robin sat on the handle of a fork seemingly just deserted by Rowan's hand. "I loved her," Andrea thought. "How could this happen?"

Her shoulders began to ache from the tenseness of waiting but when Newt's shout came from below it shocked her to her feet. She listened at the door to his rage and feared that he would kill Rowan, but Mathew's voice interrupted, reasoning, soothing as when he talked to a panicked sheep. Newt's shouting quieted but now a wailing began, inhumanly high, like a tortured animal, and it curdled Andrea's blood. Finally it too stopped. Silence. She heard Newt run from the kitchen and out the front door. She heard his feet on the gravel heading toward the road.

Downstairs Mathew's voice rumbled gently on and then Rowan laughed, a lilting, carefree sound that sent icicles up Andrea's spine and set her teeth on edge. She thought she heard the bleat of a lamb. Then silence. Rowan began to sing. Andrea listened, mesmerized, to the familiar words. When the lullaby was interrupted by the coaxing and chirps of a mother to her baby it was more than she could bear without biting her knuckle to stop from screaming.

Weighed down by a grief that encompassed more than just the one night's tragedy Andrea helplessly looked out over the fells. Something of the night before stirred in her memory. Something she had noticed but paid no heed to at the time. In the kitchen a shiny box had gleamed from a shelf that could easily be reached. Andrea forced it out of her mind and wished she'd never seen it. Not now. Not now.

Newt finally returned, and soon afterward he appeared in the garden carrying a small bundle which he took to the farthest corner where no one ever went. Andrea watched, hand over her mouth, as he dug a hole. It took only a few minutes, such a small cavity, and then he laid his burden in it and shoveled the soil back on top.

Andrea's head ached. "You're all crazy!" she muttered. "Poor little creature never had a chance. No one in the outside world even knew he lived. Poor Rowan! Poor little Sting! Poor Newt! Look at him standing over that pile of fresh earth. He's crying! Oh God, he looks so small and alone." And somehow the punk's grief affected Andrea more than anything else and tears streamed down her cheeks. She left the window and went through the motions of making her bed, all the while acutely aware of the sound of a shovel patting down wet earth.

CHAPTER TWENTY-FOUR

The day was empty. Nothing moved in the garden. Even the birds seemed to avoid it and there was no sign of the cat. Andrea tried to convince herself that things needn't change. Rowan would still work among the cabbages, and the birds would come back. Yet she knew Rowan never would be the same for her. But there was still Mathew! Dear, wonderful Mathew! Thank God she'd kept him separate. Never thought of him downstairs during the day. Never wondered what he did. He belonged to the moor, that different wonderful world that had no connection to everyday life. In her mind he was always out there waiting for her. And she would join him again tonight.

Rowan's laughter startled her and when it was followed by the strumming of a guitar and two voices softly intermingled in Newt's lullaby, Andrea forgot to breathe and stared immobile at the ceiling. The singers were beneath her window, and it was as though she was being forced to look out. Everything warned her not to. She refused to move. But the sweet song called until finally she obeyed its summons.

Rowan, wrapped in blankets, sat in a chair taken from the living room. In her arms was a bundle she alternately rocked and hugged. Horrified, Andrea looked toward the grave in the corner. It appeared untouched.

"Look, look at 'im smile!" Rowan cried and the music stopped. "Look, Newt, look! And he can talk to me!" She tipped the bundle. "Mama," it said.

Cuddles had done that. Long ago porcelain Cuddles from Andrea's childhood.

She rushed to the bathroom and threw up.

When Mathew came for her he carried the lamb snugly under one arm. Neither spoke about the tragedy. They never had discussed anything that happened in the house.

When they reached the edge of the flock Mathew put the little animal down and it stood calling, straining into the darkness. Andrea heard nothing, but the lamb apparently did because it began to run, leaping and bounding stiff legged until it disappeared.

Andrea laughed.

"'E's a lucky un," said Mathew.

"He sure is." Andrea took Mathew's hand, pressed it against her cheek for a moment, then they separated to check on the sheep which tonight were dotted all over the pasture.

The distress of the past twenty four hours slid from Andrea like scales. Her step was light as she wound her way among the flock and she recognized the ewe they had saved from wire, the lamb with the black foot that had almost drowned, and all the other lambs that grew stronger every day. What a miracle it was for her to have been able to help them and become part of their lives! She, like the wind and the grass, the limestone and the bracken, the rabbit and the curlew, belonged here. This was her world. Mathew had given it to her and she knew and loved the very taste of it, every sound and smell, every sensation under her feet and against her skin. "Thank you," she whispered. "Thank you!"

Fog was closing in. She must find Mathew. But why was that ewe circling up ahead? Andrea ran and leaned over a stillborn lamb. Another dead child. All her happiness dissolved into tears that flooded uncontrollably, draining the strength from her body.

Feeling him beside her she turned and buried her face in the rough fabric of Mathew's trouser leg. She felt his arms encircle her, lift and then hold her while she wept into his chest. "There, there, Lass," he soothed, as one finger stroked her cheek.

"Things're born. Things die. We can only love 'em, care for 'em, while we're able. We've no choice about death. It comes to all." He rocked her gently, and Andrea felt his warmth healing her as it had that lamb on their first night together. Her sobs lessened and finally stopped.

"There, there." Mathew stroked the hair back off her forehead. "The lamb were not meant to be, y'know. Maybe 'twere best it died."

"I know." Andrea whispered, knowing they spoke of Sting.

"Coom, I have summat to show thee."

By her hand he led her on an unfamiliar track, through fog that turned to mist and back again, until they reached a peak on which a cairn appeared to float in a cloud. After a short pause Mathew led her into this cloud and they moved in a white soundless void like a pair of spirits. It could have been an hour or a minute before Andrea made out a looming shadow which, as they drew close, proved to be a cluster of large rocks. Mathew led her between them into a cave. A private place of utter peace.

"This were my hideout when I were a lad." His voice could have been a thought in Andrea's mind. "Only Mother knew about it. I used to think there were a healing magic here."

Andrea knew that the comfortably hollowed rock she sat on had been placed there by that boy of long ago and she imagined him sitting as she was now, looking to where mist swirled like a cooling salve. Mathew's hand lightly rested on her forearm as he lowered himself beside her.

"Tell me about Robert."

She stiffened, but Mathew's fingers closed firmly, painfully, allowing no refusal.

"Not the tales you told me afore. There's something hurting you like Rowan's baby did her. Tell me."

And so she began. Tentatively at first, then it poured out, the whole story from the first time she met Robert and saw the photo of Lesley. All the adventure and romance, the dreams and the pain. The avoidance and distancing. The death and the last request that brought her to Yorkshire. Above all she told about the "deal" and how its conditions had ruled her life. Now and then there were things she couldn't quite remember—things that seemed to twist and change in the telling to melt like snowflakes on her tongue. In the end she was left with confusion and frightening, unanswered questions. She looked pleadingly at Mathew. Several times during her story she had felt him about to interrupt, but in the end he had just listened. Now he only murmured, "Eh, lass, Eh, lass."

Andrea rested her forehead against his shoulder. Nothing but the steady thump of his heart, then somewhere deep inside her a seed germinated. A hope that perhaps he understood something she didn't. Andrea put her arms around Mathew and hugged as hard as she could.

The fog toward the East was lightening as they arose to go. Never once did she doubt Mathew's ability to lead the way home even though she could see nothing but a white wall, wet blades of grass and bushes that all looked alike. Then they were at the back gate.

CHAPTER TWENTY-FIVE

Rowan came into the garden around noon carrying her "baby". Rocking it, singing to it. Andrea watched and wondered where on earth the boy had found the doll as the new mother put it down and ran to pick a flower to bring back as a gift. "Look, Sting, isn't it beautiful? It's for you. The whole garden's for you!"

Andrea closed the window and moved her chair to the other side of the room. She closed her ears to outside voices and longed for night.

And finally it arrived.

The moon was full—a spotlight that lit their way. Andrea watched her and Mathew's shadows merge and part with casual intimacy as they walked. Sheep picked at the grass as though fooled into thinking it daytime, and a group of lambs bucked and frolicked, playing king of the castle on a pile of stones. Andrea's inner self laughed at their nonsense as light-footed and happy she climbed beside her lover. When they reached the top she dropped his hand and began to run. She raced into the moon, her flying feet, with a sixth sense of their own, avoiding snares and holes.

Then there was Robert.

"You devil, how did you get here?" she laughed as she flung herself without a thought toward him.

His laughter joined hers as he swung her around and around.

"Where have you been?" she accused, panting when she stood on her feet again.

"I never left you," he said.

Andrea lifted both arms toward the moon. "I'm drunk!" And she breathed in the sparkling air again and again as though to absorb enough to keep forever. Remember this moment, she told herself. Remember. A star shot across the sky.

She turned toward the man beside her and saw Robert's eyes laughing at her, yet even as she smiled back, she knew it was Mathew. Yet Andrea felt no disappointment, it was as though he and Robert were one and the same. She reached for his hand and together they stood looking out across the moon washed moor.

When they parted that night Andrea put her arms around Mathew and, for once not caring about being discovered, they held each other close in the dark hallway. "Eh, Andy lass," he said into her hair, and his whisper sounded unbearably sad.

CHAPTER TWENTY-SIX

An insistent feathery tap forced Andrea to open her door earlier than usual next morning, and when she did, and was met by Rowan's naked, light grey stare, her mouth went dry. Trying not to look at the doll tucked under the girl's right arm she took the silently proffered breakfast tray.

Rowan's mouth split into a grin. "Green today for Sting and me." Rowan flopped her braid over one shoulder to show the shining emerald ribbon on its end then lifted the doll to show the twin around its neck. She looked at Andrea, waiting for appreciation.

"Yes, yes," Andrea mumbled. "It's lovely. Where do you get them?"

"Newt, of course. Says a beautiful lady deserves a gift every day. And now Sting too, 'cause he's a beautiful baby. Kiss him."

Andrea recoiled from the doll face thrust toward her, blue eyes open in a sightless stare.

"Kiss 'im. I remember you helped me born 'im. You were kind to us."

The face came closer and Andrea touched the hard cold cheek with tight, wanting to scream, lips.

The doll was snatched away and Rowan scampered down the hall with it. At the top of the stairs she paused to wave, then continued down.

"Mama. Mama." Andrea heard from far away.

Bile hovering in her throat, she set the food aside and sat on the bed watching tree branches scratch the sky.

Distant pounding. Sounded like the front door but no one ever knocked there! Thump, thump again. Footsteps crossed the downstairs hall. Women's voices. Familiar voices. It sounded like... it couldn't be... the sisters? Andrea opened her own door a crack.

"She's not up yet." That was Newt speaking.

"Her son wrote us. Said he'd got a postcard with Faws House on it. This house. He wrote but heard nowt. Says he's worried about his mum."

Of course... that card she'd bought in Farrington. No wonder the house had seemed so familiar. How stupid of her. Must have been taken long ago...

Newt was saying something she couldn't quite hear. Something about her not wanting to be bothered.

"But it's not like Mrs. James. She always answers letters."

Andrea shrank back. Those damn sisters. How dare they come here!

Newt came thudding up the stairs. Andrea wanted to hide but stood glued to the floor, awaiting the inevitable.

When the punk barged in and closed the door behind him Andrea was surprised to realize that she would much rather have him up there than the sisters.

"You know those bitches?" he hissed.

Andrea nodded.

"You mun get rid of them. Now listen. I'm going to be in the kitchen with those ashes and if I hear you tell them women owt I'll dump 'em fast. Go. make 'em clear out. Nosey buggers." He glared with all the menace he could muster but Andrea could see that he was afraid. She wanted to laugh. If he only knew that the sisters were much more of a threat to her than he could ever be. She didn't want to go down—see their pinched faces and bird-bright eyes again. But Newt was pushing her.

He ran past. "I'll be listening mind," he said over his shoulder then, "She'll be down in a minute," to those two.

Realizing she was still in pajamas Andrea threw on some clothes, all the while hating the fact of those two being in the

162

hall, snooping, and perhaps finding their way into the back garden.

She ran downstairs, hair wild and still buttoning a wrinkled shirt.

Two nightmares stood in the open doorway, motionless but for their heads which swayed back and forth, looking for her. "Eh, Andrea, is that you? My word, Sister, is that really Robert's wife?"

The despised bird-faces peered at her, and she became dizzy with loathing.

"My goodness, Agnes, I do believe it is. She hasn't half let herself go! Whatever have you done to yourself, Andrea, and whatever came over you to hire that dreadful creature who answered the door?"

"What are you doing here?" Andrea held on to the door handle.

"Why, Leslie wanted us to find out if you were all right." Effie rustled about in her raincoat pocket for a tissue. "He wrote us that you never answered his letters. You always do." She pinched the end of her nose with a kleenex, then rubbed vigorously leaving it like a tumescent boil between her sallow cheeks.

Agnes sniffed and took over. "Of course we shouldn't have bothered ourselves, not the way you treated us last, but we realized you were upset, with Robert's last request and all." A smirk pulled her mouth askew. "In some ways we were surprised you hadn't suggested it yourself."

"Well, you can see I'm perfectly all right so you can leave. I'll write to Les."

"Les?" The protest came in a chorus.

"Why yes. I think Les sounds much better than some stupid girl's name, don't you? Good-by now."

As one they reached out and began to push against the half closed door, their faces and necks a mass of straining cords. "Blaspheming the dead. Evil woman. Have you given her Robert's ashes yet? Have you? The dead will punish you if you haven't. Lesley's waiting for him down at that churchyard. Lesley Clayton is waiting!"

"Go!" Rage tripled Andrea's strength and she slammed the door and leaned against it listening, first to a moment's silence, then to their fading footsteps.

A small sound alerted her to Rowan's wide-eyed presence in the shadows near the kitchen. She hugged the doll and murmured to it excitedly.

Andrea ran upstairs.

Tattered inside she tried to pull herself together by remembering last night's moment of perfect happiness, but it danced out of reach. "Oh, Mathew." She looked up at the boy above her bed. "Please, Mathew, tell me nothing will change." She looked out at the moor, into the garden, and up at the trees. All so familiar. I do love this place, please don't make me leave, she prayed to the curlew that hovered against the blue sky.

Something moved in the corner of her eye. It was Rowan creeping around the corner of the house, dollbaby clutched to her breast, something shiny dangling from her fingers. What was she doing? For a moment Andrea mourned the pregnant girl, so magically fey, whom she had cared for so deeply. That innocent child prisoner who had changed overnight into an aberration. Look at her now, moving like a thief, going behind the shed. She must be hiding from Newt for some reason.

Andrea turned away and picked up her writing pad to begin a letter to Leslie which, unlike some others, he would receive.

An engine burst into a roar close by and dropping the paper she dashed back to the window to look out just as Mathew burst from the kitchen, Newt close behind. Clouds of smoke poured from the Escort's exhaust as the engine revved and raced. Andrea could see Rowan's head as she peered intently through the windshield while the car fought and strained to escape the weeds that had grown around it. Terrifying images flashed through Andrea's mind of what would happen in a moment when the car was free to gain momentum. It leapt forward. Was almost past the corner of the shed, dragging vines behind it.

Andrea leaned out the window as Mathew ran straight to the passenger door and yanked it open. He flung his upper body inside, reaching for either the key or the brake, but at that instant the car broke lose. Turning too sharply it hit the corner of the shed and in horrifying slow motion Andrea watched the door being forced shut against Mathew's struggling body. She couldn't move. Couldn't breathe.

Newt, already at the other side, hurled the girl out onto the ground, climbed in and jolted the car into reverse. Mathew, released, fell limply into an inert heap.

Now Andrea ran as fast as she could, although it seemed like crawling, down the stairs and outside. Newt kneeled beside the old man who was whispering, "Don't fret, lad, I'm all right." But he was white behind his beard and didn't move.

Andrea crouched on his other side, aware of Rowan behind them whimpering over and over, "I was taking Sting to see mother. They said she was waiting at the church. I wanted to see mother."

"Get an ambulance," Andrea said. "Quick, Newt, you've got to!"

Newt hesitated, looking down at the crumpled figure, then his face twisted. "Aye," he said, and was gone.

Andrea tugged off her sweater and spread it over Mathew, then she kneeled helplessly beside him watching his nostrils move with frail, small breaths. "Oh, Mathew, please be all right. What would I do without you? We'll get your farm, replant your mother's garden. Oh, Mathew!"

Rowan had wandered over to the bench by the kitchen door where she rocked and soothed her baby.

Mathew moved, just a fraction, and his eyes opened. "Andrea, listen carefully. It's all right. You made me young again, but I'm old." His tongue ran around his lips and Andrea leaned close to hear. "It's about Lesley."

"Don't talk now. Rest, my love, the doctor will soon be here. Dear Mathew, please..." Andrea glanced toward the gate but there was no sign of help.

"Andy, listen to me." It was a command and she leaned close again. "'T'was different than you think. Lesley had a child, a daughter, four years afore your Robert came. Them sisters saw him—wealthy American. Figured to get rich and rid of Lesley in one. Made 'er hide the child, get 'im to marry her, take her to America. But he bought this house—planned to move in. 'Twouldn't do. Sisters harped on and on at 'er, forcing her to make him take 'er away. She never loved 'im. Couldn't bear to leave her Rowan. Drove her car into the wall of that bridge out there. Rowan were meant to die too but she just got damaged." He licked his lips and closed his eyes a second. "I were Lesley's friend, since she were a nipper. Liked to wander with me like you do. She talked to me but I couldn't save 'er. Sisters played on Robert, made 'im feel guilty. Still got their bit off 'im." It had all poured out in a frantic rush and now exhausted, Mathew closed his eyes. He ran his tongue over his lips again. Andrea waited. Dazed. His skin was grey and his voice a mere breath. "Andy, Lesley would never hurt you. T'other night, your story, your truth was like a mirror. Things got turned around for you, twisted, like the lass and her dollbaby. Think on it well." He took her hand and opened those clear blue eyes that even now smiled at her. "Be good to the boy and know, Andy lass, you were the one he loved." His eyes closed and he sighed.

Oh please, Newt, hurry!

They came. Men in white pushed her aside and surrounded Mathew. Andrea and Newt couldn't see him and were made to feel intruders as the men did their work. Eventually they straightened. One came over and after a moment's hesitation chose Andrea as the one in authority. "Old chap's gone, I'm afraid. Much shock as anything at his age. We'll take 'im. Let us know when arrangements have been made." He took out pencil and paper. "Can you tell me 'is name?"

When nothing seemed forthcoming from Andrea he turned to Newt.

"Mathew Hornesby," the boy said with a flash of defiance.

The man wrote then put the tip of the pencil to his lips. "Mathew Hornesby. Not the same as murdered 'is brother over some land? Big thing in the papers some twenty years back. "Most wanted" wasn't he? Reward out for 'im. Thought 'ed skipped the country."

"'E come back."

"Police'll be interested to hear this. Everyone figured he'd be dead by now. How old was he anyway?"

"Go. Leave us be." Newt's voice broke and the men went back to load the body onto the stretcher.

Andrea had been listening as though to a TV show. This had nothing to do with her. Mathew would be there tonight, waiting for her. He'd never leave her, she knew that.

Then they started to carry him toward the ambulance and she ran forward and looked down. The man lying there was frail and small, and so very old. No, this wasn't anyone she knew. She stepped back and they moved on.

Andrea looked up at the moor climbing toward the sky and imagined Mathew striding there, strong and ageless, caring for his beloved sheep. She was numb—afraid to move lest the pain begin.

Rowan, on her bench hummed the lullaby over and over.

Newt came up beside Andrea, swishing a clump of grass against his thigh. They stood not speaking, then he blurted. "Guess they'll come for 'er next. Saw 'em looking."

"Did he kill his brother over the farm?"

"Aye. Loved the place 'e did. Did 'e show it to you?"

"Me?"

"Aye, at night when 'e took you out."

"You knew?" Andrea looked in surprise at the boy beside her. Short and so thin, arms folded across his chest in an effort to look strong but he trembled and his face was pale and taut. And oh what anguish in those eyes! She had the sudden urge to take him into her arms and comfort him as if he were her own son—as she needed to be comforted.

"Course I knew. Couldn't keep you in all the time. 'Ad to

167

keep you afraid of me though or you'd not've come back." He spoke in a monotone as though scarcely conscious he spoke at all. "You'll 'ave me put in jail now?"

"You kept Mathew hidden here from the police?"

"He'd a died in prison. 'E'd done so much in 'is life. Was like a dad to me. Only one who told me my music was good. Encouraged me to play and loved to listen. Only grown up as ever cared about me, 'e was."

The sheep had come down the hill and Andrea watched as a lamb bleated and ran to its mother, butting her hindquarters off the ground as he drank. He's almost too old for that, Andrea thought. They were all getting big now. She looked around the garden and up at the window she had stood at so often. She'd never been out here in daylight.

Neither of them knew what to do. There seemed no reason...

"Newt. Newt lad. Are you going to rehearse this morning? Sting wants to hear you."

They both started at Rowan's interruption. "In a moment, in a moment," said the boy.

"Why do you keep her captive?" Andrea asked, stroking the leaf on a nearby tree.

"Captive? Oh aye, you would think that. Pop's grand-niece she is. Through the son of the man he killed. Boy got a kid called Lesley preggers then took off, and when she killed 'erself Pop took care of the kid she'd tried to kill with 'er, sending money when he was away. But 'er little mind were damaged in the crash and got worse. When Pops took off after the murder they put 'er in a home. A terrible place near Bradford. Somehow, wherever 'e was 'e heard and came back. The two of us sprung 'er." He stopped, with a little remembering grin, then swallowed a choking in his throat. "They both stayed safe here. No one ever comes. Got a reputation for being haunted, you see. But then you come. I got the note so we was ready. Had to keep you or you'd a had both of them locked up."

"Oh, Newt..." Andrea wanted to say she wouldn't have but

she knew that at that time she would. "How did you ever support us all?"

"I make money. My group's going well. Got a gig most nights."

Rowan seemed content now, chattering to the doll, humming bits and pieces. She looked so pretty, so pure—so angelic.

Newt was looking at her too. "She kept wanting me to let 'er get an abortion. 'Eard one of my friends talking about it. Didn't understand, of course, poor thing. Maybe I should have let 'er."

Side by side they walked into the kitchen. They sat across from each other at the table. The cat padded from one to the other, mewing.

Newt stood up and got it some milk, then he dragged a chair over, climbed on it and carefully lifted the gold covered box down from the shelf. "'Ere, you can 'ave 'im back now."

Andrea put the box on her lap. Full circle, back to the duty she had come to perform, as though nothing had ever happened. As though there were no Mathew. Dear Mathew, where are you? Oh Mathew, Mathew! Her throat and chest felt as though she had swallowed cement which was rapidly, painfully solidifying. How could someone be here one minute then just gone? Her fingers stroked the box beneath them. Oh Mathew! Oh Robert! I'll go crazy. I can't bear this, I can't.

"I'd not 'ave tipped 'im, y'know."

"What?"

"I'd not 'ave dumped them ashes like I said I would."

Andrea stood up and passing behind Newt, paused with her hand on his shoulder for a moment then, carrying the box, she went upstairs.

She stopped in front of the mirror and faced the woman Mathew had discovered. It was a surprise to see her still strong and youthful; she'd fully expected to have lost herself too. "The truth is in the mirror," Mathew had said. But everything was opposite in a mirror.

No good thinking. Do something. Anything. She looked around, seeking escape, then she abruptly picked up the gold box and ran downstairs. At the foot she glanced toward the kitchen where the boy sat backward in a chair, resting his chin on his arms. His eyes watched her, but he made no move to prevent her departure, only his hands let go and drooped hopelessly downward.

CHAPTER TWENTY-SEVEN

Andrea walked down the overgrown driveway and all the time something inside insisted this was all a dream. Soon she'd awaken and eat the breakfast Mathew brought, then perhaps Newt, and a still pregnant Rowan, would sing and laugh in the garden below. She'd look forward to darkness, climbing high on the moor after checking the sheep with her strong, beloved friend. She'd tell him about this nightmare. "Eh, Andy lass," he'd say." 'Twas only a daft dream. Aren't we always going to be together? Who'd fix our valley if I went away?"

Andrea hurried along the road. A car swished past, then some young people on bicycles. She passed a cottage where a woman worked in the garden with a radio blaring from inside the open door.

"Good morning, Missus." The woman looked at her, eyes curious.

Andrea was almost trotting, the box awkward and heavy in her arms, sunlight catching on it and occasionally blinding her. She mustn't hesitate, impetus must carry her through. When this duty was done it would be the end.

She reached the churchyard gate, rushed up the shaded walk and around the corner to where Lesley waited.

"Oh, sorry!" She'd almost run into a workman. He picked up a shovel lying in the grass and went back to join another man who labored, already knee deep, on a new grave right next to Lesley's.

Andrea stood dismayed. She couldn't spread the ashes with them there! She backed around the corner of the church and leaned against the wall to think. She could hear the clatter of shovels and the men talking.

"Strange Mathew coming back 'ere to die, though when I think on it I'm not surprised."

"Aye, 'e did love Starwell. Allus come back no matter where 'e went. 'E could tell some stories in the pub in t'old days."

"I never blamed 'im for what he done. Reckon 'e 'ad good reason."

Andrea heard the striking of a match.

"Aye. Allus liked 'im, I did. Reckon 'e was the only true friend that lass under yonder 'eadstone ever 'ad. Good we can place 'im next to 'er. Allus one to care for summat 'urt or weak, 'e were."

"Funny thing, I almost thought I saw that lass Lesley, a minute ago. Bumped into a woman looked just like she'd a done by now, 'ad she lived. Kind of wild like—pretty."

Unconsciously Andrea's fingers ran over her cheek, and her other hand tightened on Robert's ashes.

Noticing a door beside her she turned the iron handle and pushed it open, releasing a gust of chill, musty air. As she entered the semi-dark church all the habitual reverence learned in youth returned. Automatically she bowed her head toward the altar and sidled into a pew. She kneeled, but instead of praying she looked up at the Christ in the stained glass window and felt a wave of fury. "How could you have been so cruel? Striking such a vicious deal so I suffered all those years. I trusted you!" Her voice echoed, awakening sleeping shadows.

The compassionate eyes of the bearded man gazed tenderly down at her. He carried a lamb under one arm.

Andrea began to quiver. She stared deeper and deeper into that familiar face, struggling to understand. "Mathew?" she whispered.

Slowly she sat back on the bench, touched the box beside her, eyes still on the window. That Christ could never have wanted to hurt her, there was no hint of cruelty there. Somehow she'd been mistaken. Then what had happened? Confused and more lost than ever Andrea rose to go.

The men were still working when she left the churchyard. and she hardly noticed anything on the walk back along the road, over the bridge and around the gate. The house door remained open as she had left it.

The sound of weeping drew her to the kitchen where Rowan sobbed and hugged her baby while Newt tried to comfort her. "Nay lass, don't take on so. I'll still take care of us somehow, you'll see."

Andrea, unnoticed in the doorway, watched Newt clumsily stroke the girl's hair. His face was pale without makeup. How could she have been so afraid of him. During all that time why had she never seen through his desperate facade?

"I'll buy you a satin ribbon bigger than any you ever had," he promised.

How much of his meager earnings had all that ribbon cost? No wonder he had no warm clothes.

Rowan's tear blotched face studied him earnestly. "Scarlet?" she asked.

"Aye, whatever you want."

"Please play for us now."

"Aye lass, if you like." As Newt reached for his guitar he saw Andrea standing in the hall. For a moment he hesitated as though to say something but then he picked up his instrument and sat in the chair opposite the one where Rowan had settled herself and her doll-baby.

He began to play. Something soft and beautiful that reminded Andrea of the wind in the grass and rippling streams on the moor. It brought back the smell of Mathew's jacket, the soft touch of a lamb's muzzle, the stroke of a finger along her face.

She sat down on the bottom stair. That tune changed to a livelier beat so her foot couldn't help but move, and she felt the beginning of a smile in her heart. Mathew was right, the boy was talented. His music should be heard. Not just that rock stuff he earned his money at now. She looked from his intense face to the entranced Rowan's. There must be a nice place she could go to and be well looked after—with a garden and friends. Newt could help choose it. What a burden that poor kid had carried, what sacrifices and decisions he must have made to protect the two people he loved. Andrea stood up. You're free now, Newt, and I'll help you however I can. She'd have to choose her time and put it carefully so he'd be sure to accept.

Her arms ached from holding the box and she carried it up to her room and set it on the dresser, then she sat on the chair in front of it and looked at the photo she had seen more often than her own face.

Lesley looked sadly back at her. Lesley who had killed herself rather than marry Robert and leave her daughter. Then why had Robert wanted his ashes put where they weren't wanted? He was too proud for that. Suddenly Andrea was on her feet, digging through her suitcase for the folder of important papers. Finding it she pulled out one from among others, smoothed it and really read it for the first time. "I wish that my ashes be put to rest with my one true love, that we may at last be in peace together. May she finally believe that I love only her."

"You were the one he loved." Andrea heard Mathew's voice, and understood what he meant. He had seen what she had refused to see through all those years. Andrea faced herself in the distorted looking glass. "You fool. You stupid, blind fool! There was never any deal. There was no need for one! Oh, Robert, I'm so sorry!" Andrea pressed her face to the gold box, and hugging it saw again the wonderful husband who had loved her too much. "My poor darling, what did I do to you!"

*   *   *

Andrea put the last photo of Lesley in the bottom of the old dresser and closed the drawer, then she gently put Robert's ashes back into the suitcase for the trip home along with the needlework of Mathew and his dog. The calico cat purred around her legs. She stroked it. "I'll miss you little one, you and

Newt and all of this." She looked out at the moors and knew they would always be a part of her. Whatever happened in her future she would be able to smell the wind and the heather and the sheep...

Must get moving, there was a lot to do. After Mathew's funeral Rowan must be settled and Newt made legal caretaker of Faws House, with good wages to help him in his career. He must get a good agent... he was bright, he'd know what to do. Then the trip back to California where Robert's son awaited his mother. Suddenly Andrea longed to see her boy more than anything else in the whole world.

ABOUT THE AUTHOR

Vancouver Island native Jil Plummer has trained horses in England, acted off-Broadway in New York City, worked on a banana plantation in Jamaica, and coordinated a clown show on ABC in Hollywood. While married to a photojournalist she traveled on many assignments throughout the world. She has also taught English as a second language. Jil has currently published two books (Caravan to Armageddon and Amber Dust) and has many more stories to tell.

For more information, please visit: www.jilplummer.com.

www.ingramcontent.com/pod-product-compliance
Lightning Source LLC
Chambersburg PA
CBHW071242130626
46556CB00003B/1125